COG

K. ceres wright

**DOG STAR
BOOKS**

Published by Dog Star Books
Bowie, MD

First Edition

Cover Image: Bradley Sharp
Book Design: Jennifer Barnes

Printed in the United States of America

ISBN: 978-1-935738-43-5

Library of Congress Control Number: 2013935019

www.DogStarBooks.org

Thank you to God and my loving family, without whose support this book would not have been possible. I love you.

Thank you also to my Seton Hill mentors: Timons Esaias and Steven Piziks.

Thank you to my Seton Hill critique partners: Kim Howe, Rachael Pruitt, Amanda Sablak, Erica Satifka, and Maria V. Snyder.

To Heidi Ruby Miller, Jennifer Barnes, and John Edward Lawson: Thank you for everything.

To Michael Carolan: Thanks for telling me a published book trumped an MFA.

To Les Brown, Tod Lackey, and Dan Trotter: Thanks for writing with me.

To Karen Arnold, Derrick Collins, Denise English, Tracy Holmes, Regenia Jones, and Renee Moore: Thanks for your undying support.

FOREWORD: COG

by Christopher Paul Carey

I've long believed that one of the best means of effecting enduring change in society is through the creative arts, whether in the form of fine art, music, poetry, film, television, video games, or literature. Politicians and lobbyists can stir up emotions and lawmakers can determine policy, but it is the artist, trained to intuit the subconscious patterns in the complex matrix known as culture, who best reflects the voice of society and, sometimes, helps call the future into being.

While I don't believe K. Ceres Wright sets out to change the world with her debut novel, *Cog*, neither do I think it is a coincidence that her protagonist, Nicholle Ryder, hails from a background in the fine arts. One needs an artist's eye to take on the system, to perceive its weaknesses and strengths so they can be leveraged into a creative solution for society's problems.

Classical art and music might at first seem out of place in a near-future cyberpunk thriller. Wright knows well, however, that contrast is one of a writer's most effective tools, both in terms of theme and as an instrument of world building. The rich allusions to painting, sculpture, and music that suffuse *Cog* not only weave a skein of originality and uniqueness over Wright's hi-tech future; they also create a contradistinction whereby the reader can more easily make sense of and slip into a world of "pakz" and "skeemz" and "spiraling in." Wright, a nominee for a Rhysling Award by Science Fiction Poetry Association, defines the world of *Cog* not through wordiness, but, like any good poet, through structure. We don't need to be told what medinites are; Wright trusts us to understand from context.

Wright also knows that art by itself cannot effect change. Therefore, Nicholle Ryder is not just an art connoisseur; she is also a recovering drug addict who has descended into the gritty underbelly of the enclaves far beneath the glistening skyscrapers of her family's wireless hologram monopoly. Though a member of the upper class, she is streetwise and knows how the abandoned, poverty-stricken suburbs of her world's fuel-cell economy prop up the very people who despise them. Despite its exotic technologies, the world of *Cog*, with its lived-in feel and shades of gray, operates much like our own, illustrating that the human equation remains constant even in the face of scientific progress.

But what ultimately makes K. Ceres Wright's *Cog* such a satisfying read is that it works as well as a thriller as it does social commentary and technological extrapolation. Its careful balance of corporate intrigue and breakneck action makes it the perfect debut release for Dog Star Books, whose motto—"Science Fiction That Goes for the Throat"—could not be more appropriate. So whether you're a fan of William Gibson's *Neuromancer*, Ridley Scott's *Blade Runner*, or simply good old-fashioned science fiction adventure, *Cog* has got you covered—and then some.

Christopher Paul Carey
Seattle, Washington
December 2012

Christopher Paul Carey holds a B.A. in anthropology and an M.A. in Writing Popular Fiction. He is the coauthor with Philip José Farmer of *Gods of Opar: Tales of Lost Khokarsa*, and the author of *Exiles of Kho*, a prelude to the Khokarsa series. His short fiction may be found in such anthologies as *Tales of the Shadowmen*, *The Worlds of Philip José Farmer*, and *The Avenger: The Justice, Inc. Files*. He is an editor with Paizo Publishing on the award-winning Pathfinder Roleplaying Game. Visit him online at www.cpcarey.com.

chapter 1

Perim Nestor stood watch over Arlington from a curved window office in the American Hologram building. A scrim of clouds obscured most of the evening sky as commuters headed home, yet a roseate sunset tinged the underside of the grey, offering hope of a sunny tomorrow. Reflections from the streets below, clotted with the red of brake lights, danced merrily on nearby buildings.

Perim abandoned his watch and took up residence against a credenza along the opposite wall, arms folded, jaw clenched, waiting for the coming storm. He did not have to wait long.

"You're joking, right?"

William Ryder stretched the skin between his eyebrows with his thumb and index finger, then formed a fist and slammed it on the table in front of him. He stood up, hunching over the edge of his father's cherry wood desk. The owner sat on the opposite side, glaring. Light from a squat, burnished pewter lamp threw up blurry shadows on the metal paneling.

"Right?"

"Wills, sit down!" The stentorian voice of Geren Ryder echoed in the large office. The bones of his face set like ice, holdovers of the Last Glacial Maximum. Salt-and-pepper hair framed a mahogany canvas.

His son was a mirror image, only more muscular, with the coloring of polished sepia.

Perim Nestor remained silent. However spartan the office, it reflected more than the green and brown décor. It reflected the multi-trillion-dollar company that Geren Ryder had built from scratch. And he was used to being listened to.

Wills sat down, but the tenseness remained. He hovered on the edge of the chair, ready to spring. Geren continued, his voice now measured and calm.

"I didn't know Perim was my son until last week. After I confirmed it, I've been...coming to grips with the implications."

"Confirmed?" Wills said. "So it's been confirmed that you whored around on my mother. As if I hadn't already known. And what do you expect me to do? Jump up and say, 'I've always wanted a brother'? Shed heartfelt tears and give him a slap on the back?"

Silence. The ether froze, like hanging mist on a December morning. Perim drew up his lips and met the flinty stare Wills leveled at him. He couldn't blame the man. Heir apparent to a wireless hologram empire and presto change-o...a long-lost older brother appears.

"Does Nicholle know?" Wills said, eyes still riveted on Perim.

"No. She's busy recreating the Prado in Anacostia. I didn't want to distract her. It's her first full-scale exhibit," Geren said.

Wills relaxed somewhat, straightening and placing his arm on the desk. *Mrs. Arthur Knowles and her Two Sons* looked on the proceedings from the wall behind Geren. In the painting, Mrs. Knowles was sitting on a couch, one son clinging to her as his hand rested on a book. The other son lay wrong-way on the couch, barefoot, his hand on his chin, as if contemplating some mischief.

"I don't want anything material...no money, no stock. I just want acknowledgment," Perim said.

"Acknowledgment!" Wills sprang from his seat. "And why do I have a hard time believing that? On the eve of my father announcing his retirement from American Hologram, you just *happen* to show up."

Wills approached Perim, jabbing a finger in the air between them.

"I've dealt with drug dealers, pimps, and CEOs, and I know bullshit when I hear it. It's all the same. You want something. Something like American Hologram."

Perim straightened. "I head my own accounting firm. What would I need with your company?"

"Why settle for a little power, when you can have a lot?"

"Is that your life's motto?" Perim stole a glance at Geren. "In that case, you'd better watch your back, Father."

Too late, Perim noticed the oncoming blur of flesh, the carpet rising to meet the side of his face. His next view was of a sideways Potomac River through the curve of the picture window. The reflection of neon pinks and blues undulated in the invisible waves and careened like a slow-motion merry-go-round. Wills' feet left his field of vision. Wind chimes whispered as he exited through the magfield.

"I should have told you he boxed in college," Geren said, matter-of-factly.

"No shit," Perim said, only it came out sounding like, "Oh ih." His head spun, mental function a whirlpool. He edged up on one elbow, then leaned against the credenza and slid upright. The room slowed.

"You'll come to work for me. I'll make you a vice president, but you'll have to prove your mettle," Geren said. "Especially to Wills. He can be a hothead, but he respects skill."

"I have my own—"

"Company, yes. That has a quick ratio of point seven eight. How long do you expect to stay in business running those numbers?" Geren arose and began packing a briefcase that lay open on the desk.

Perim pulled himself to standing, gripping the credenza. "We just scored a large contract with the defense department." He rubbed his jaw, hoping there would be no bruise.

Geren guffawed. "If you call forty million a large contract. Look, it's settled. I just sent in the approval. Let your second run the company and you report here first thing in the morning. But...we will wait on the acknowledgment until after I announce my retirement." He closed the case and hefted it off the desk. "Come prepared to learn. See you tomorrow."

Wind chimes echoed again as Geren disappeared through the doorway. Perim smiled to himself. *This is going better than expected.*

✿

Perim's new office smelled faintly of antiseptic, as if it had just been cleaned the previous night. And perhaps it had. He hadn't gathered much information about his father in the short time he'd known him, but he gleaned that he was, above all, a man of action. Perim sat in the leather chair behind his desk and whirled around once. A blurry view of downtown Arlington whizzed by.

A woman appeared in the middle of the room and eyed him suspiciously. He jumped slightly, then realization caught up. A hologram. He cleared his throat and pulled up to the desk.

"Yes?" he said.

"I am Jamie 3.5. If you like, I can appear in male form."

"Ah, no. You're fine as is," Perim said. She was not beautiful, which would have been a distraction. In fact, she had rather a square chin, he thought, and closely-set eyes. "I assume you're everyone's assistant?"

"Correct."

Perim waved his hand in a circular motion. "What, ah, what are you running on?"

"Quantum computer, Cognition 1.5."

"Huh, I see. Okay, then, what do you have for me?"

"For your schedule today, you have a ten o'clock and a four o'clock with Geren Ryder. Also, would you like me to order lunch for you, or will you be eating out?"

Perim leaned back in his chair, fingers intertwined behind his head. "I will be eating out. And no need to make reservations. Thank you, Jamie."

"You're welcome." Jamie stood stock still, her eyes looking past him, blank for a few seconds. Then she focused on him.

"I have updated data. Geren Ryder would like to move your ten o'clock to nine thirty, as an unexpected meeting came up," she said.

"All right. Let's see, that's in…five minutes," he said, his gaze shuttling to his periphery. "I'll be there."

"I'll inform Mr. Ryder."

She disappeared.

Perim wondered what Geren would say. After 35 years of non-acknowledgment—claiming he didn't know—what would he have to say?

He arose and made his way to Geren's office, following the directory he'd tapped up. Geren's door was a wide gothic arch whose magfield displayed a red wooden door beneath a bloom of crosses bottony in stained glass. A bit pretentious, Perim thought, but he'd seen worse. The previous night, the magfield held no decorative motif, just the wind chime sound effect.

He stepped through into the Spartan green and brown office from the night before. Not to his surprise, Wills stood in front of the picture window, his fists jangling change in his pockets as he rocked smoothly on his toes and back. Nervous energy bound tight. Geren sat at his desk, thumbing through financials. He looked up at Perim's entrance.

"Ah, there you are," Geren said.

Wills spun in Perim's direction, his gaze like a shot from a splinter blaster.

"Geren. Wills."

"Getting acclimated?" Geren said, thumbing closed the company statements.

"Yes. Jamie 3.5 has…" Perim nodded. "…been most helpful."

Geren cut a glance at Wills. Tension radiated from him like a bride the day before the wedding with no reception hall.

"Sit or stand, it makes no difference," Geren said, seemingly exasperated.

Wills' gaze tracked back to the picture window and he continued rocking, as if ignoring the both of them. Perim crossed his arms and leaned against the wall next to the magfield. It opaqued, solidifying to a dark grey, denying entrance to passersby.

"I'll get straight to the point," Geren said. "I have made Perim a vice president of AmHo. He will report to you, Wills…"

Wills momentarily stopped rocking, tensed the fists in his pocket, then resumed.

"…and I'm counting on you to be fair-minded. His birthright is not of his making. Now, as for succession, since we are family owned and managed, Wills is next in line, then my daughter, Nicholle. Although I'm sure she wouldn't want the job. You will be on a six-month trial, Perim. After which, if you have performed satisfactorily, you will be added as third in the line of succession. That is my decision. Any questions?"

Perim waited for Wills to lodge a protest, but none came.

"And on what criteria will my performance be based?" Perim said.

Geren waved a hand, as if the criteria were common knowledge. "Oh, ability to manage people, knowledge of the industry, ability to spot trends and leverage them, the usual. I'm sure Wills can work with HR to come up with some performance standards and go over them with you."

Wills grunted. Perim couldn't tell if it meant yes or no.

"Wills!" Geren said.

Wills turned to face Geren, his expression blank. "I'll meet with him tomorrow." A slight smile. The kind painted on clowns. Perim shivered.

"Is that it?" Perim said. He lifted off the wall and stood, hands in pockets.

"You'll be assigned a bodyguard," Geren said.

"Already got one. And I trust him."

"Very well, just give his information to the security department. And don't forget our four o'clock."

"Wouldn't miss it," Perim said, trying to keep the sarcasm out of his voice. Failed. The magfield turned transparent and he left, glad to shake off the tension that had built in the room.

He bee-lined for his office, opaqued the door, and sat in the middle of the semi-circular couch at the darkened end of the office.

He brought up his node and scanned the day's news. One article caught his eye: "Two American Hologram subscribers were found unconscious at their homes while cogged in. Anomalies were found in their systems…" *Drugs.* "…and both remain in a comatose state." The company had issued a statement saying that wireless hologram is completely safe and that they would work with the authorities to determine what had transpired.

Interesting.

Perim bounced around on his own node, then the company's, looking for its own anomalies. He tested the limits of his access—Startup folder, yes; Registry folder, no—which confirmed what he had expected. He pinched the skin behind his ears and squeezed out a BackdoorRTY.3 sepsis, then uploaded it to his node. He programmed it to remain in place for twenty-four hours, then transfer to the company node and conduct its own investigation.

His door chimed and Perim hurriedly closed down his node. It faded into the air before him. He tapped thumb and pinky once, and the magfield switched from dull grey to a school of freshwater fish.

Wills stepped through and Perim rose to meet him. Wills paused, eyeing Perim as if sizing him up for a suit fitting. The skin on Perim's neck began to itch.

"I'll need to map your brain for executive access to Cognition," Wills said. He held up a small, black device. "Won't take long."

"Is this necessary?" Perim said.

The clown smile again. "Afraid so."

"Very well."

Perim allowed him to place the device on his forehead, which hummed softly, then pinged after about twenty seconds. Wills recovered the device, scanned the results, and nodded.

"Good scan. Ah, is eleven o'clock good for tomorrow?"

Perim nodded. "My schedule's free, so far."

"Great. See you then."

At that, Wills turned and left.

○

Perim checked the time in his periphery—3:30. Tiredness stole over his body and mind from attending meetings, talking to employees, glad-handing fellow managers, and reading corporate documents. He edged back in his seat and activated the massage feature. Warmth suffused his neck and back as vibrating, kneading balls wended their way up and down his spine. Muscle tightness alerted them to a need, and they lingered in the middle of his back, where tension had knotted. He allowed himself to close his eyes, relax, and fall into the chair's embrace.

"Emergency meeting called. Please attend. Room 718."

Perim jerked upright. Jamie 3.5 stood before him with a newly acquired halo of orange that blinked staccato.

"What's going on?" he said, hands gripping the arm rests.

She merely repeated the previous message. Perim groaned and turned off the massage.

"This had better be good."

✿

The conference room was filled with managers Perim had met earlier in the day, and one or two he hadn't. The meeting was being led by Chris Kappert, head of IT. His face expressed pure shock. Some managers next to Perim were bandying about the words, 'ambulance' and 'embezzle.'

The hell is going on?

Chris finally spoke, his voice cracked and emotion-laden.

"If I could have your attention, please."

The room instantly fell quiet.

"I'm afraid I have some rather bad news. Geren Ryder has fallen ill and was taken by ambulance to Washington District Hospital. I will be going over there myself shortly to get more information. As of now, we don't have any idea what is wrong, but rest assured that he is in capable hands.

"In another matter, which may be related, William Ryder is currently missing. He is not answering cogs and has not been seen in the building since 10:30 this morning. There is also…a substantial sum missing from the cash accounts."

Murmurs rose until Chris put up a hand for quiet.

"There may be an explanation for all of this, but as of now, if you are contacted by William Ryder, please refer the call to HR. His node has been locked, and if he asks anyone for access to corporate documents, as I said, alert HR immediately. I'm afraid that's all the news I have for now. I will keep you updated through the executive node as soon as I find out anything else."

"Who's going to run the company?"

The question came from a woman in the back. She had spiky red hair and a morgue-like pallor.

"As you know, we are family owned and managed, which makes Nicholle Ryder the present head of company."

A small collection of groans rose up.

"I will approach her about taking the position, but if she refuses, then it would fall to the Board of Directors to appoint someone."

Perim's jaw tightened, but he kept his peace. He should be next in line, but he wasn't on the list. Not yet. But with Geren and Wills out of the picture—an interesting turn of events—he made an urgent note to consult with an attorney.

chapter 2

An orange sun hung low in the sky, beneath long bands of dark clouds, as if the sky were winking one last time before the sun sank beneath the undulating waters of the Anacostia River. Flecks of black dotted the scene—birds catching dinner by the dying light. Their cries were carried along the wind, then faded as the air currents shifted. The light gleamed on the marble of the Prado's Ionic columns that fronted long rows of paned windows. Statues ensconced in their rectangular recesses stood guard next to barred archways.

Nicholle Ryder stood out front, waving her hand as if creating the scene by magic.

"No, the columns by the front door are Doric, not Ionic. You'll have to reprogram," she said.

Haedn Gupta jabbed a finger in the air, keeping a list on his node.

When Nicholle's father agreed to sponsor the Prado recreation, he lent her Haedn from American Hologram's optics department, who at first denigrated the project every chance he got. After their display of a partial beta version at a kindergarten, however, he became an ardent supporter. The excited way the children reacted to works of art they normally would have shrugged at had drawn him in...had drawn them all in.

"We had to make some adjustments to account for a more narrow staging area, so just go through the museum and make a note of what needs changing and we'll do everything at once," he said. "And this time, you're getting a cut-off date, Ms. Perfectionist."

"So you say, Haedn, so you say. What about David?" Nicholle said as they strode through the front door. "Tell me his backside is as beautiful as the day it was sculpted."

Haranguing the Gallery of the Accademia di Belle Arti had finally resulted in the holographic rights to the statue, *David*—a feat she wouldn't let her boss forget. She had even beat out the Louvre.

"Take a look for yourself." He gestured toward the towering statue to his right. "I put him just inside the front door, to keep anyone in line distracted," Haedn said. "People are less prone to frustration if they're not bored."

Nicholle nodded approvingly as she traversed around the statue, admiring the finely sculpted figure. Hair curled about his face, brow folded in tense anticipation. She came to a halt halfway around.

"I always took you for an ass...woman." Reya Connors, assistant extraordinaire, came up beside Nicholle, punching the air with her finger. Blonde hair tied back with a scarf, 5'3" frame draped with a grey herringbone suit. Matching pumps. A model of efficiency.

"You're as funny as a Blue Period work," Nicholle said. She stood back to admire the view. "It looks so life-like," Nicholle said.

"I don't know. David's not exactly well-endowed. Perhaps Michelangelo didn't want to linger there too long."

Talking to Reya was like talking to middle school boys. Eventually the conversation came around to sex or genitalia.

"Are you diagnosing Michelangelo with penis envy?"

"I'm just an executive assistant. What would I know?"

"We could make it bigger," Nicholle said.

Reya chuckled. "Yeah. Wait—what? I was joking. The purists would have our heads on a pike. Not to mention the Gallery of the Accademia. The contract states—"

"Yes, yes, exact likeness and all that, but controversy means longer lines. And it's not a violation if it's a malfunction. Haedn! Add four inches to the front," Nicholle said. She would deal with the fallout later.

"Hold on. Cog from Seppotia," Reya said. She walked toward an alcove and spoke in low tones.

Haedn's concentrated focus melted into a look of consternation. Then his face darkened to the color of an aged cabernet and he began to sputter and shake. "What? The statue of David is a masterpiece. No one—"

"We'll get more publicity, which means longer lines. The longer the lines, the more money," Nicholle said. "Which means a bonus for you."

Haedn's mouth hung open and his eyes rolled upward and froze in their orbit, like the top car on a Ferris wheel. Then he reanimated, looking around for anyone within earshot.

"For one day," he said in a loud whisper. "That's it!"

Nicholle gave him thumbs up. Haedn had a wife with expensive tastes and twins on the way. He had probably been up all night trying to figure out a way to afford Quattrocellini cribs and strollers.

Reya returned, hands on hips with a laser-beam gaze, which always meant bad news. Nicholle braced herself.

"Seppotia from the Guggenheim rejected our offer for the holographic rights to Kandinsky's *Accompanied Contrast*. I told her she could lick my cat's balls," Reya said. Efficiency by Vassar, mouth by U.S. Navy.

Nicholle closed her eyes and rubbed flat the sudden grooves on her forehead. "Tell me you didn't say that."

"Well, not exactly. But I was in projection mode."

That must have been an eyeful, Nicholle thought. Nicholle had had words with Seppotia before—civil, yet underscored with mutual hatred. The words, 'luddite,' and 'artistic purity,' were bandied between them.

"Reya, I know Seppotia can be difficult, but she's leaving next month, and after she's gone, we're still going to have to deal with the Guggenheim. Try and be civil."

Reya gave her a stony look but stayed silent.

"Come on. Let's check out the Yebedor oils," Nicholle said. She walked around to the statue's front and collected a perturbed Haedn. They walked through the Renaissance, crossed the Enlightenment and Victorian Ages, and entered the Contemporary Age. Abstract oils, originally two-dimensional, hung suspended in air in distended form. Statues moved twenty degrees clockwise, then returned to their original pose. Museum workers moved in and out among the art, setting up ladders, installing diodes, calculating algorithms.

The oil paintings of Tre Yebedor occupied a room off of the Contemporary one, filled with blazing colors, hazy curves, and effervescent lines. The collection contained twenty oils.

"No, no. The arrangement is all wrong," Nicholle said. "I want them in chronological order." She pointed to the paintings in the order they should go. Reya punched and dragged the air, moving the oils into the specified order.

Chris Kappert. The name glowed orange in Nicholle's periphery, signaling an incoming cog.

"Chris Kappert? I haven't talked to him in a year. Hold on, Reya," Nicholle said. She tapped her ring finger twice against her thumb, answering the cog. Chris's transparent image hovered in front of her.

"Yes?" she said. He had changed his look. A year ago, he had dreadlocks and sported wrinkled shirts. Now he wore closely cropped dark hair and a navy suit. Green eyes ringed in hazel reflected a world-weariness that was not often seen in men his age.

"Hello, Nicholle. Nice to see you again. Unfortunately, I'm afraid I have bad news. Your father has fallen ill and has been taken to a hospital."

Her arm froze in mid-sweep. Chris's voice dissolved into a clanging dissonance in her mind, blending with the hammering of the museum workers. The oranges and blues of abstract art morphed into a blurred, whirling landscape where gravity did not fasten.

No, it can't be.

"Wha—What...did you say?"

"Your father's been taken to the hospital. He's in Washington District hospital. I'm there now in the nanosurgery waiting area," Chris said.

Only Nicholle heard him, but Reya rushed over and helped her onto a bench.

"Are you all right?" Reya said.

"He's not dying, is he?"

"Who?" Reya said. Nicholle squeezed her arm to silence her.

"I don't know yet. The doctor hasn't come out to talk. And, we have issues to discuss. Try to get here as soon as you can," Chris said.

"We don't have a thing to discuss other than my father." She tapped her ring finger twice against her thumb and Chris faded to black.

✿

Nicholle skirted past an elderly couple and bounded up the green marble steps of Washington District hospital. She reached the top, ran through the magfield—emblazoned with the blue-and-yellow seal of the hospital—and butted her way past startled patients. She tapped open a directory, which unfolded before her in a holographic display of green and black. She sprinted toward the elevator.

"Nanosurgery, nano…third floor." Nicholle repeated the finger taps and the directory faded. She slipped between the closing elevator doors and almost ran into a stout woman wearing a turban. The overhead speaker sounded, "Please step away from the doors."

"Third floor," she said. The 3 lit up in response. She stood just inside the door, tapping her foot. *C'mon, c'mon. I can't believe they brought him to a public hospital.*

Her attention was diverted by a holo-ad moving across the wall in front of her. Two pictures streamed by, side by side, one of a woman in a bed, tubes running from her arms and legs to bags of liquid hung on tall racks, the other of a woman walking down the street, smiling. Beneath the ad scrolled the words: From this…to this. Medinites®. Changing the Way You Heal.

Insipid elevator music played overhead, homogenized versions of last year's songs, threatening to send her over the edge of impatience.

She rocketed out of the elevator when the doors opened and sped down the hall toward the surgery wing. A large, blonde woman sat behind a desk, greeting visitors, and looked up expectantly as Nicholle approached.

"Can I help you?" she said.

Nicholle ignored her and strode through the magfield, which was decorated with a waterfall scene, and into the waiting room.

Chris sat on a settee by a large window that faced the Ministry for Purlieu Security. The slowly shifting blues of the walls and the muted greens and beiges of the carpeting were designed to calm edgy relatives, but had no effect on her.

"Where is he? What happened?" Nicholle stopped in the middle of the waiting room floor, demanding answers.

Chris walked over to her. His grey eyes held a warmth that Nicholle had never witnessed, and his somber countenance reflected a concern she didn't think he possessed.

"He's still in surgery. As for what happened, he was walking down the hall when he suddenly collapsed. No warning sign of chest pain or headache. Nothing. He just collapsed," Chris said.

"What did the doctors say?"

"They haven't spoken to me yet. But the nurse said the surgeon should be out in a little while."

"Where's Wills?"

"Your brother…is on his way."

"So what do we do? Just wait?"

"That's all we can do. Have a seat."

Nicholle threw her purse in a green chair by the window and sat down.

"How's work?" Chris said.

"Fine." She wished the waiting room had soundproof partitions. Worrying over her father was stressful enough without having to tolerate Chris, as well.

"Just fine? I heard you were working on a new exhibit. I know you love creating art displays."

She made no reply, but Chris pressed on.

"In fact, I was thinking of coming down—"

"Can you quit with the small talk? I'm not in the mood."

Chris shrugged. "Have it your way."

Nicholle saw movement in her periphery. A woman's head emerged from the magfield to surgery. The head remained suspended in a sea of white, soon joined by the rest of the body, adorned in a maroon anti-contaminant suit. Nicholle jumped from her chair and rushed toward the doctor, just stopping short of bowling her over. She fought the urge to take the doctor by the shoulders and shake the answers out.

"How is he?" Nicholle said.

The doctor drew up her thin lips until they practically disappeared.

A shot of pain burned in Nicholle's chest. The background noise of the hospital faded to a distant droning and her mind clouded over. *It's worse than I thought. God, don't let him die, don't let him die.*

"I'm Doctor Lars, head of nanosurgery. Mr. Ryder is in a coma. We've administered fluids, vitamins, and pralaxinine, and programmed his medical nanites to stimulate the cerebrum, which rules consciousness. So far there's been no reaction, but it may take some time. All we can do is wait for now and see what happens."

"How long do we have to wait?" Nicholle said. "Can I see him?"

"I don't know how long it will be before he regains consciousness. And, unfortunately, I'm afraid you cannot see him at the moment. Rest assured, we're doing all we can." She paused. "You are the next of kin?"

"Yes, I'm his daughter, Nicholle Ryder."

"I just want to inform you that your father has a living will that stipulates if he remains in a coma longer than five days, he is to undergo medinite-assisted euthanasia."

"What? Are you insane? I'm not allowing that. I don't care what the will says. Do you know who he is?"

"I'm well aware of his identity, Ms. Ryder, but that doesn't change matters. Living wills have to be respected, whether they be of presidents of companies or janitors." Dr. Lars adopted a smug look. "As I said, we're doing all we can. I suggest you all go home and get some rest. We'll call as soon as anything changes." With that, Dr. Lars walked back through the magfield, disappearing into a sea of white.

Stunned. At both the doctor's disrespect and the time limit. Five days. The euthanasists had gone too far. The laws they had pushed through Congress were supposed to be for those who couldn't afford health care, to cut down on suffering. But they had gotten weak-willed officials to kowtow to their demands, and now they were all paying the price. "I don't believe this. What the hell? Euthanasia? Did you know about this?" She leveled a gaze at Chris.

"Me? I knew nothing about your father's will."

"Oh, c'mon. You were up to your elbows in my father's business. You knew everything he did, from what he had for lunch to what color tie he would wear the next day."

"Jealous of that?"

Nicholle's hand landed hard on Chris's cheek. Heads jerked in their direction. Her hand smarted, but she refused to flinch. She'd wanted to do that for a long time. Chris kept his head to the side for a few seconds, then eased it back around. Nicholle turned away.

"Euthanasia." Hot tears spilled down her cheeks and onto her sweater. The muted greens and beiges of the waiting room coalesced into a blur. A knot cinched her throat. Chris came over and took her by the shoulders as he led her to the settee.

Her tears dried, her medinites tending to her body's crisis. A sense of calm enshrouded her and the fog began to lift from her thoughts. But she wanted to grieve. *Let the tears come.*

"Why isn't Wills here yet?" Nicholle said. "He needs to be here." Next to her father, Wills was the only person she had left in her immediate family. Their mother had been killed in a plane crash when she was two. After that, she had lived with the fear of losing her father, the reason Nicholle had tried to stay up late, waiting for him to come home from work when she was little. She'd always fallen asleep before he got home, though. Wills had always gone to bed on time, on the dot.

Chris sat next to Nicholle. He took her hand in his and spoke in a soft voice.

"There's something you need to know about Wills. And I'm sorry to be the one to have to tell you this at such a time."

"About Wills? What are you talking about? Is he all right?" She grabbed his arm, digging her nails into his suit jacket. Her heart began to pound again. If something had happened to him, too…

"I'm sure he's fine."

"What do you mean you're sure he's fine? You said he was on his way. What are you talking about?"

"We haven't seen Wills since ten thirty this morning. And there's a large amount of money missing from the company. Fifty billion dollars. All calls to him are diverted to an answering service."

"What? Fifty billion?" Nicholle said. "Why didn't anyone tell me?"

"We were hoping it wasn't what we thought. When was the last time you saw him?"

"About a week ago. We took the scramjet to Mexico for Jera's wedding."

"How did he seem?"

Nicholle fought hard to think back to the trip…past recent events, past worry, doubt, and guilt. He'd been more quiet than usual, but, nothing out of the ordinary. In classic Wills style, he had managed to inform her of various esoteric facts. They rattled around in the back of her consciousness—Nazi SS officers had their blood type tattooed on their left armpit; the only rock that floats is pumice; Pierre Picaud inspired *The Count of Monte Cristo*.

"I need a drink," she said. She left her node address on the hospital's 'Notify Immediately' list. They'd cog her if anything changed, at least that's what the doctor said. Dr. Lars would probably activate the euthanasia process tonight if given the chance.

"A drink?" Chris said. "I don't thi—"

"I don't want to hear it." She snatched up her purse and headed out the magfield. The closest bar was Malabo's, one block over. Chris caught up and escorted her, silent, though one glance told her he was holding back a spew of disapproval. *Fine.* The last person's approval she wanted was his.

She cogged Wills the whole way there, hoping he would answer and say it was all just a joke. But he didn't pick up.

✿

Malabo's typified the encroaching African-Chinese subculture—walls adorned with large wildlife batiks, flanked by Chinese tiger paintings. The blend was almost seamless, one of the reasons she kept coming back.

"Whiskey shot, double," she said. She took a seat at the end of the bar, facing the door. Old habit. The bartender smacked a double shot glass on the counter and filled it with the golden liquid. She cogged the cost, tapping her thumb on her temple, then downed the glass. She had almost forgotten the burn. Closed her eyes and relished the remembrance.

Chris cleared his throat. She ignored him until the last of the burn faded.

"So why do you want to know how Wills seemed? If you're asking whether he told me he planned on stealing company money and leaving town, then no. He didn't," she said. "So what do you want from me, Chris?" He must have wanted something, otherwise he wouldn't have spent so much time with her, especially in a bar.

"In addition to current…incidents, it's not yet widely known, but American Hologram is about to be audited by Innerworld Revenue. We've sold off some assets to keep the ratios up and managed to keep it out of the media so far. But it's going to hit when we file the quarterly reports. And when it does, I think we'll get less of a negative impact from our subscribers if there's some family continuity."

"Continuity? What are you talking about? You want me to take over the company?"

Two small dents cleft between his eyebrows, alerting her to the gravity of the situation.

"Yes, at least for a little while."

"Well, well. So now you want me? Will it be for longer than three weeks this time?"

"I know you're not bringing up the internship issue," Chris said. He averted his gaze, toward the window. The dents deepened.

"If there's one thing I learned from that, it's that people rarely change. If ever."

"You were in over your head and you knew it."

"I needed help, not a push out the door."

"You were kissing your father's ass too much to worry about what you wanted."

"That coming from the expert on kissing my father's ass."

The warmth in his eyes at the hospital had dissipated like alcohol in blue flame. "You found a job you loved. Why are you blaming me for that?"

"It was the way you did it. You enjoyed it. Like some sadistic pervert."

The bartender glanced over and sucked his tooth. A warning. Chris ignored it.

"Bullshit. The longer it dragged out, the harder it would've been. You wanted to wait around, let your father tell you what and who you should be. *I* knew that job wasn't you."

"And since when did you become the expert on me?" She strained her voice to keep from yelling. "My relationship with my father is none of your business."

"You know what? We can sit here all day going round and round. Meanwhile, your father's in a coma and the company's about to tank. I'm asking you, on your father's behalf, to step in and help save what he started. If we go down, thousands of people will lose their jobs. Now either you're in or you're not. Your choice."

Nicholle swallowed, hard. "You've changed from the happy-go-lucky techru you were a year ago."

"I grew up," he said.

Feeling suffocated, Nicholle got up and pushed past him. She walked to the bar front and leaned against the window, pressing the side of her forehead on the cool glass. It had started to rain and beads of water snaked down the pane, leaving thin trails. Cars crowded the airways, signaling the beginning of rush hour.

Everything was hitting close to home, her father, her brother, the family company. The last thing she wanted to do was take on more responsibility in her state of mind. She walked back and paced in front of the antique jukebox.

Sometimes she couldn't help but wonder where she would be if she had stayed on the streets. If her brother hadn't given her the ultimatum that he would clean out her accounts if she didn't sober up and come home.

The old feelings surfaced: fear, revulsion, guilt. Fear of dying in a cold back alley with no one finding her body for weeks afterward. Revulsion at her addiction, at her perceived weakness at not being able to 'just say no.' Guilt at having left, without warning, those whom she'd befriended. *Even Tuma.*

She remembered feeming pakz and skeemz when she used to get high. The pakz delivered a more visceral feeling, the direct rush of drugs injected into the blood stream by medinites. You still saw reality, but you didn't care. Yet, there was that needling prick in the back of your mind, reminding you that your reality was what you were going to have to deal with when you came back.

Skeemz, on the other hand, stimulated the imagination beyond one's natural ability, creating a feeling of frenzied euphoria. Your reality would wait forever. Seemed as if the programmers discovered new and different ways each week to simulate an endorphin rush. Customized programs cost more, but offered to change the way you perceived your world.

I wonder how I'd perceive all of this on skeemz?

She sidled back to the bar, arms crossed. "I'm a curator at a holographic museum. No one is going to take me seriously," she said.

"I'll handle senior management and the auditors," Chris said. "You just look like you're in charge. That should be easy. You've acted before."

She squeezed her thumb until the medinites lowered the barriers. The flush of the whiskey warmed her, and a gleeful disposition eased across her mind. It'd been a long time.

Responsibility, duty...what did it really get you in life? Boredom. But her father needed her. She'd disappointed him before; she wasn't about to do it again. She released her thumb and the flush subsided. Duty called.

"I'll do it," she said.

"Good. I'll tell the employees and assign you a bodyguard."

"Bodyguard?"

"Standard issue for a corporate executive. I'll send him over this evening. You two can meet and set up a schedule."

"But—"

Chris tapped Nicholle on the side of her shoulder with a fist. "Thanks, Nicholle. See you later."

Nicholle's stomach coiled into a knot as she watched Chris rush out the door. What did she know about running a wireless hologram service provider? Her company internship had been an admitted—never to Chris—disaster. But she wouldn't need to know anything. Chris would do all the work. *Right?*

She pulled out a cigarette and tapped the end on the edge of the counter. It lit up. She liked her nicotine the old-fashioned way. She sat down at the bar and crossed her arms, mashing her thumb under her elbow. The flush returned. *Welcome home.*

chapter 3

Walking into Riklo Castor's office was like walking into a gamer shop—a new feature every day. Today's works of art were a holo of Taliesin West, *Dogs Playing Poker*, and *The Thinker*. The building and dogs stood off to the side, while the statue sat in the middle of the room. Nicholle stepped through *The Thinker*. Riklo didn't know much about art, although he pretended he did. Nicholle let him have his fantasy.

Riklo looked up when she approached his desk. He wore last year's look of slicked-back hair and a skinny tie. As he was tall and wiry, the tie made him look thinner.

"Nicholle. Good. I just cogged Henri at the Louvre. We're still in the running but they won't make a decision until next week. Now as far as the Prado is concerned—"

"Riklo, I have to leave," she said.

"For where, the Louvre? The personal touch. Good thinking." He shook a finger in her direction.

"No, the job. I have to leave the job."

He gave her a double take.

"What are you talking about? Did you get a better offer from another museum? I'll match it. Plus a bonus." He stood up, boring his knuckles into the exposed wood from underneath a scattered hodgepodge of wi-papers. "You can't leave me now. We have an exhibit coming up that I'm hoping will raise money from the patrons. Especially Mr. Garampo."

A 2D Diego Rivera print hung on the far wall. *The Flower Vendor* looked at her and Riklo with interest as she sold another batch of calla lilies to a girl in pigtails.

29

"My father's in a coma," Nicholle said. She sat down and leaned her head back on the chair, browsing the orange and blue bas relief ceiling tile, amazed that she was still coherent after leaving the hospital. The events of the day had left her unable to think beyond basic daily functions.

"A coma? Fema," he cursed. "I'm sorry, Nick. I didn't know," Riklo said. "How'd it happen?" He sat down in the leather chair and folded his hands across the desk, like a first-grader waiting for recess.

"The doctors don't know. They can't say when he'll come out of it." She neglected to mention the living will stipulation. It was enough of a nightmare. She didn't want to relive it. "The head of IT asked me to take over as acting president, for the time being, until my brother gets back from out of town." *If he gets back.*

"Can you handle that, with everything going on?" He sounded condescending, as if eager to hear a no in reply.

"It's not about me anymore. If I don't go, the company may lose more jobs than if I do go. Believe me, I wouldn't leave if I didn't think I had to."

Riklo may have had no sense of art, but he was a decent boss. He'd been given the job by his father, who owned the museum, so it wasn't as if he would be fired if he didn't meet the bottom line.

"It'll be a lot of stress, crazy clients, dumb employees, inept management." One side of Riklo's mouth turned down. "Look, I'll just give you family leave. If it doesn't take longer than six months, your job will be here when you return."

It made more sense than quitting. "Thanks, Riklo. I really appreciate that. I'll hand my files over to Reya," Nicholle said. She smiled at him, then left.

✿

Reya wasn't in her office and Nicholle didn't feel like cogging, so she uploaded her instructions on the upcoming Yebedor exhibit and saved it to Reya's node. Nicholle was sorry she would miss opening night. The exhibit was a social commentary piece illustrating the growing divide between the classes. She had studied Yebedor in college and admired his work. When she lived on the street, the meaning behind the paintings became clear. Funny that—a revelation through a pakz-induced high in which all the world's issues were solved in a moment's thought. And then with soberness came crushing reality.

The transition to corporate life would unsettle her, she knew. Remembrances of boring meetings, angry shareholders, and disgruntled employees flitted across her mind. She forced the thoughts from her head.

This time it will be different.

Riiight.

She was going to pack her things, but decided to leave them. She'd be back. Small though it was, her office held a lot of good memories—like the time Reya had bought Riklo a blow-up doll and was waving it around in the hallway while his father looked on, furious, from the conference room. Nicholle hadn't known Mr. Castor could curse like that. But they'd all had a good laugh after he left. Then there was the time they landed the rights to the drawings in Chauvet Cave. They'd celebrated for days after.

"I shall return," she said to herself. Grabbed her Quatrocellini bag and headed out. Her heels on marble echoed in the long, empty hallway. The Artists Hallway. Holos of painters, sculptors, and architects lined up on either side, watching as employees came and went.

Albrecht Dürer, *Self-Portrait at 28*, hung at the end of the corridor, one of Nicholle's favorites. She paused for a last look.

It's not the last time. Keep telling yourself that.

His eyes seemed sadder than usual—or was it her imagination?

"See you, Al. I still think you're hot."

She walked out into the night. Tall trees silhouetted against the moonlit sky hunched over the edge of the parking lot, as if hunting prey. Her car's proximity sensors unlocked the door and turned on the engine. The door swung up as she approached.

"Good evening, Nicholle," the car's smooth baritone voice said.

"Evening, Max," she replied.

"Will you be driving tonight?"

"Nope, it's all yours. Been a rough day."

"Destination?"

She hesitated. Guilt had nagged at the back of her mind since the drink in Malabo's. She'd officially fallen off the wagon, but given the circumstances, she thought it understandable. Not that she was making excuses...

No, that's exactly what you're doing.

"Where's the next, closest twelve-step meeting?" she said.

"1725 Rhode Island."

"A.A.?"

"Yes."

"Take me there."

✿

A host of cars huddled under the dome of St. Matthew's Cathedral, testament to the number of those come to call. Nicholle had remembered her first twelve-step meeting—had expected to see nothing but barely recovering, recently high addicts who'd been forced into treatment by well-meaning relatives. Instead, she'd found people from all walks of life, in various stages of recovery. Some a few days sober, others decades. And they'd all welcomed her. It had felt like a familial embrace, one that she'd never had.

Max rolled to a stop and opened the door. Nicholle climbed out and pulled up her coat against the night chill. A few stragglers were wending their way around to a side entrance, and she hurried to fall in behind.

Technically, she was an addict, not an alcoholic, since her drug of choice was pakz. She drank, but not to the point of drunkenness. She'd relied on the pakz to take her over the edge. Way over.

"Hey," she said to the two stragglers. "Is this open or closed?"

Closed meetings were for A.A. members only, or for those who had a drinking problem and wanted to stop. *Open meetings* were available to anyone. She'd faked it before, just to get into a meeting she felt she needed. Replaced "pakz" with "alcohol."

The man on the left, dressed in a thin leather jacket and tight jeans with a chain that ran from the back pocket to his belt, spoke first, albeit briefly.

"Closed."

The woman on the right came across as more sociable. She wore a brown patchwork velvet skirt that fell to the floor and a green sweater. She had a tangle of brown curls with blonde highlights that framed a narrow face.

"First time?"

"First time here, not first at a meeting," Nicholle said.

"Well, welcome. My name's Daria. This here's Jim."

Jim said nothing, but opened the door to the church and waved them in. Nicholle let Daria take the lead, and they wound up in a small room of women. Jim had veered off, presumably to join a men's group. Nicholle eased into a chair as she nodded greetings to the others. She tapped her thumb against her index finger three times, cogging out. The small group sat at desks formed in a rectangle. Nicholle figured the room was used for Bible study.

A chubby woman with short, copper-colored hair, sporting a tattoo of praying hands on her left forearm led the meeting. After reading the A.A. Preamble and leading the Serenity prayer, she opened the floor. Counterclockwise. Which meant Nicholle was third in line.

Nicholle listened to people's personal tales of loss and recovery. When it was her turn, she crossed one leg over the other at the ankle and took hold at the juncture.

"Hi, I'm Nicholle."

"Hi, Nicholle," everyone said.

"I, ah…became an alcoholic a little over two years ago. My mother died when I was two and my father was rarely home, so it was mostly me and my older brother growing up.

"So, about two years ago I went to work for my father in the family business…only it didn't work out. I didn't quite fit in, since I was the 'artiste' in the family." She paused. "I never quite fit in. Anyway, after I was, in effect, fired from an internship, I hit the party scene, drinking and pakzing my way through D.C. and Maryland. I hooked up with a leader of a skeemz gang and cribbed in, did what I could to earn my keep. But I was drinking more than I was making, so I stole money from him to keep myself boozed and pakzed up. I knew he'd find out eventually, and I called my brother for money.

"He said he would give it to me only if I came in for treatment that he could monitor. I was desperate, so I agreed. Only I haven't seen the gang leader since. Which means I...haven't lived up to Step 9 of the program, but something tells me...I may have the chance to reconcile that."

Her gaze shuttled around the room until it landed on Daria. She had that Mother Earth aura and she looked at Nicholle with the same intensity she probably gave a mushroom burger.

Nicholle spoke on. "This afternoon, I found out my father fell ill, with only five days to live. So I went to a bar and had a drink. I have to admit, it felt good, relieved a bit of the stress. But it's good that I felt guilty enough to come tonight, cuz a couple years ago, I would have thought nothing of it. Anyway, thanks for letting me share."

The group thanked her for sharing.

✿

After she made her farewells, she trotted across the parking lot and climbed into warm leather.

"Home."

Nicholle sat, numb, behind the wheel as it crossed the 14th Street Bridge. The car continued on autopilot through the streets of Southwest D.C., snaking past tony shops and bars that spilled forth moneyed clientele. The bouquet of culinary creations of four-star restaurants wafted through the air vent, but it failed to stir her senses. Her gaze swept over the reflections of buildings undulating in the waters of the Potomac River.

Flashes of light illuminated the interior of the car driving under the street lamps. Flashes of memory illuminated her thoughts.

Nicholle tapped her index finger three times against her thumb. Prismatic colors spiraled around her, then whipped into a tight coil, bringing the scent of fresh flowers. The standard greeting sounded in her ears, "Welcome to Cognition."

"Play Tekirna Maro," Nicholle said. Tekirna's voice flooded the car, and Nicholle's senses filled with the smell of vanilla and the sights of purple and orange lights.

She checked her father's status on the hospital node, but it only blinked "Status Unchanged" in bright blue. She sank down into the seat and closed her eyes, all the way home.

Arriving at the programmed destination, the car slid under the garage door, eased into a designated parking space, and shut off. Nicholle exited and headed for the nearby transport tube.

As she rode along the horizontal track to her condo, her incoming cog light flashed purple. *Call from Tyla Porreaux.* Nicholle tapped to answer the call, voice only, and Tyla's chattering instantly filled Nicholle's head.

"There you are. I swear, you need to stay spiraled in, you luddite. We still on for dinner?"

"Listen. I really need to talk to you. Can you and Keala come over now?"

"Sure thing, pachika." Tyla's voice mirrored instant concern. "You okay?"

"I'm not sure."

"Oh, hon. Look, we'll be right over. See you in five."

Nicholle terminated the call just as the building's retinal scan confirmed her identity and the doors to the tube opened. Nicholle stepped into her great room, heels clacking on the oak flooring. Strode past the baby grand piano and round the corner to her bedroom suite. She threw her purse on the chair to the right of the door. The walls were painted crimson, accented by an open-scroll ceiling medallion. The bed stood on a dais against the far wall, draped in gauzy mesh from a canopy. Beaded pillows spilled from the bed onto the floor.

Nicholle kicked off her navy Quatrocellini shoes, doffed her suit, and threw it at the feet of the laundrobot. Its single arm with two extensions bent to pick up the outfit for deposit into the ultrasonic cleaner.

She pulled on her favorite sweatsuit. The magfield chime rang and she hurried out to the living room as the butlyr stood aside to let the guests enter. Tyla and Keala whirled into the room, chattering, rustling bags, and clanking bottles. Tyla had narrow almond-shaped eyes and wavy amber tresses that complemented her café au lait complexion. Keala had a wide-eyed innocent look that made her seem younger than her twenty-six years.

"What's wrong?" Tyla said. "You didn't sound good at all when I cogged."

"Hey, guys. Just put the stuff in the kitchen," Nicholle said. "I don't feel like cooking. Maybe we can order something."

"No, no. As much as we paid for this steak, I'm cooking it. Consider me your chef for the night," Keala said.

They gathered in the kitchen over ginger ale and cheese and crackers. Keala fired up the grill and seasoned down the steaks. The flames reflected off the red aluminum tiles, lending an intimate feel to the spacious room. Nicholle told them about her father, Wills leaving, and Chris's request. As she told the story, it resonated as someone else's, or as some cheap skeemz one could buy off the street for a pack of cigs.

"Oh, honey, are you okay?" Tyla said. She wrapped a hand around Nicholle's arm in support.

"Just kinda numb right now, you know?" Nicholle stared into the pale gold of her ginger ale.

"I can't imagine what it's like. So your father might be—?" Keala said. She broke it off and looked down at the steaks before spearing one and laying it on the fire. It sizzled, sending up a tempting aroma.

Nicholle filled in the blank. "Euthanized." It was hard for Nicholle to even say the word. "I didn't know he believed in that. I can't imagine him doing that."

"But it might be the best thing. No suffering," Keala said.

Nicholle downed her soda. "That's just it. I don't know if he is suffering. The doctors, apparently, don't have a clue as to what happened."

"I can't believe Wills just took the money and left," Tyla said. "Ass."

"He wasn't always that way," Nicholle said defensively, to her surprise. Her first memory was of her brother pushing her on a swing in the backyard when she was two. He used to defend her from Anatol, the neighborhood bully, once even getting a bloody nose for his troubles. As they grew, to help with their grief over their mother, they had called each other every day from their respective boarding schools. He used to tell her stories about their mother, so she would not forget. When they were home, their father barely spoke to them. He would creep into their room when he got home from the office to kiss them goodnight, after they had gone to sleep. She knew this because he would sometimes leave a piece of candy or some jewelry on her nightstand. Only when she grew up did she realize her father was probably working through his own grief.

"Maybe my father's lawyer would know something about his living will," Nicholle said. The idea just came to her. "Why didn't I think of that before?"

"Yeah, but will he tell you anything?" Tyla said. "Confidentiality and all."

"He'd better tell me something. And take care of this euthanasia business." The walls of her self-restraint buckled and swayed. Nicholle tapped open a line and asked for Henroi Jebted, face scan enabled. Momentarily, the visage of a man with salt-and-pepper hair in a dark grey suit appeared. He sat at a desk cluttered with e-pads, poring over one in particular. His image sprang out, sharper than reality. Upgraded diodes.

"Yes, what is it?" He didn't deign to lift his head.

"Henroi, it's Nicholle Ryder."

His head jerked up, facial muscles flickered—*surprise?*—then slid into customary placidness. "Nicholle. I was going to cog you. I'm so sorry about your father."

"Henroi, did you know about his living will? What the hell? Five days?"

"Your father made his own wills, both his living will and his last will and testament. The living will would only be viewed by his attending physicians. I can, however, research precedents regarding the challenge of a living will. Your father did not have a history of mental illness, so we can't say that he was mentally incapacitated."

"I don't care, Henroi. Do what you have to. I don't want him euthanized."

"I'll see what I can do."

"Do more than see," Nicholle practically shouted. "And another thing, Chris Kappert asked me to take over the company since Wills skipped town with fifty billion."

Henroi's cheeks darkened, as if he was personally embarrassed over Wills' behavior.

"Yes, Chris told me you would be heading up the company." He cleared his throat. "Since Wills' behavior can be viewed as criminal, you will also be in control of the entire Ryder estate. Minus, of course, the Foundation. Your father and brother still own majority shares in the company, but will not be able to exercise any rights without the Board's permission. If Wills is exonerated, then control will revert back to him. But I'm drawing up the papers now for transfer to you."

"I see," Nicholle mumbled. *Only it's not supposed to be like this.* Her father and her brother were the responsible ones who took care of the family—well, what was left of it. She was the aimless one, the screw-up.

"Fema," she said.

"Is there, ah, something wrong?"

No time for introspection.

Henroi's brows bridged, as if recreating Pangaea. "Has someone told you about Perim Nestor?"

"Who?"

Henroi's forehead slid back from his face, drawing up his eyebrows.

"Ah," he said. "Well…" He cleared his throat again. "Your father…" He slid her a furtive look. "…recently discovered he had a child out of wedlock thirty-three years ago, Perim Nestor. Your father hired him and put him on a six-month trial period, after which, if he performed satisfactorily, he would be placed in the line of succession. Third, to be exact."

Henroi's words bounced in the timeframe between hearing and comprehending, not quite completing the connection.

"Wait wait wait…what? My father had an illegitimate son, and hired him? When was this? And no one told me?"

Rage crept into her voice. The astounding number of the day's revelations threatened to send her screaming to Sheppard Pratt, begging to be admitted. The sound of Keala choking on a cracker broke through her conversation. Tyla and Keala looked at her, slack-jawed. Nicholle made a rolling gesture she hoped they interpreted as 'I'll tell you later.'

"He found out last week, confirmed yesterday. He told me he didn't want to bother you with it during your Prado exhibit," Henroi said.

"Well, who is Perim Nestor? Where does he come from? What's he like? I mean good heavens...a new brother?" She slapped a palm across her forehead.

The magfield chime rang again and the familiar whir of the butlyr followed.

"What now?" Nicholle said. "Hold on, Henroi." She paused her call and strode to the living room, half expecting a Quatrocellini purse delivery, but then remembered she hadn't authorized an entry. The butlyr semi-opaqued the magfield to allow for speech.

"Who is it?" Nicholle said. A shadowy figure hovered just beyond the door.

"Talo Spyre. I'm your bodyguard. Sending up authorization now."

Nicholle's periphery blinked red, then green as authorization was accepted. She allowed entry, and a tall man stepped through into the small foyer. He sported the brash confidence of a Mars shuttle commander, surveying the room as if ready to plant Old Glory between the cushions of the chintz sofa. Black hair waved back, stark against pale skin and watery blue eyes—a rugged handsomeness accented by a day's worth of stubble. His nanon suit iridesced subtly, taking environmental readings—from room temperature to shifts in object proximity—feeding data directly to the cortex. She'd seen the like on Tuma's personal sentry. Whoever this man was, he was top drawer.

He proffered a hand, closer to his body than social convention dictated, as if drawing her into his space. She took the bait. He shined a perfect smile; goosebumps rose on her flesh.

"Talo Spyre, at your service."

Tyla and Keala emerged from the kitchen, grinning like kids over a broken piñata. Nicholle introduced Talo and they all retreated to the living room. She messaged Henroi and told him she would call him back.

Tyla and Keala squeezed Nicholle between them on the love seat; Talo sat opposite on the chaise lounge.

"So…how long have you been…bodyguarding?" Nicholle said. She'd never had a bodyguard before and found the idea ludicrous. But she didn't want to upset protocol. She had enough to worry over.

"Ten years," Talo said. "Mostly for corporate executives."

"So…what duties will you be performing?"

He sat on the edge of the lounge, leaning forward, as if relaxing in a chair was a luxury rarely afforded. "I will plan routes, search rooms you'll be in, check the background of people with whom you'll have contact, search your vehicle, and escort you on your daily activities."

"Is all this really necessary? I mean, it's not like we've had issues at AmHo where people have threatened lives. And excuse me, Mr. Spyre, I didn't offer you anything to drink."

She fought her way from between Tyla and Keala and headed for the kitchen. "Is ginger ale all right?" she called out behind her. "I also have tea, coffee, water, and juice." She grabbed a glass from the cabinet and stood at an open refrigerator, waiting for a reply. None came.

Then two lason shots.

Goosebumps. Her mind raced, instincts leaching back from street days. She pulled open the dish-towel drawer, reached at the back, and grabbed a Semi. Footsteps. Blue heat crackled past her head and she fell back, prize in hand. She pointed and fired blindly. She took out part of the wall, but nothing else. A sliding sound, as of someone crawling on carpet, and she lunged right and fired.

A scream. *Got him!* He rolled, groaning, but twisted an arm around. His blast took out the Monet print on the wall, water lillies now a blackened hole. Nicholle fired at his back. His arm thudded softly on the carpet. She stood still for a moment, taking in the scene of a charred body lying on her dining room floor; she slid down the wall, scarcely believing what transpired…like 2D film noir. *Tyla!*

"Tyla!"

She ran to the living room and took in the gruesome scene.

Too late.

Blackened heads lolled at odd angles, bodies slumped to the side. Tears welled and streamed. She slid down the wall until she reached the floor and cried.

When the oppression of three dead bodies nearby became too much, she cogged Chris. His face hovered before her, sporting a bored expression that quickly changed to shock once he took in the scene.

"The hell happened to you?" he said.

Seething fury boiled up. "Your bodyguard tried to kill me! He killed Tyla and Keala. What the fuck, Chris!"

Bewildered look this time. "What are you talking about? Are you okay?"

"I can't believe you're asking me if I'm okay when you just tried to have me killed!"

"I didn't try to kill you. The bodyguard was Perim's choice. I told him I was getting you one, and he said he'd handle it. What happened?"

"What happened?" she repeated, with a helping of sarcasm. But it was as if her mind refused to relive recent events. Perhaps she was in shock and couldn't remember if she wanted. She closed her eyes. "I got off the phone with Henroi to answer the door. The bodyguard came in, introduced himself, and we sat down in the living room. I asked him about his duties, then I got up to go to the kitchen to get him something to drink. And that's when…"

Tears streamed again.

"Stay there. Don't cog anyone. I'll be right there."

○

She sat on her bed, wishing she had a pakz when the bell rang. Nicholle ran to the door, checking authorization on the way. Opened the magfield, pulled Chris inside, and opaqued it.

"Oh, my god," he said. He surveyed the scene, holding a hand to his mouth. The odor of burnt flesh had dissipated somewhat, but still pervaded the room. Nicholle had never shot anyone before; bad odors were the last thing she had expected.

"The hell do we do? Call the cops?" she said. The idea of calling the police on oneself railed against her sensibilities as an ex-drug dealer. But she would do it to keep from being charged with murder.

Chris still stood, running his hand over chin stubble.

"Chris!"

He jerked. "I don't know, Nicholle," he said, irritably. "I've never had to handle burnt bodies before."

"You're acting like this is my fault."

"Don't be—Hold on. Cog from Jamie," Chris said. He tapped open the line. "Yes?…What? Wait, you can't be serious. Hold on." He turned to Nicholle. "Turn on the HV."

"What? You want to watch holovision, *now?*"

"Jamie said Perim just announced that we stole twenty billion from the company," he said, motioning for the HV. It clicked on. Hovering before them was a company photo of Chris in a navy suit next to one of Nicholle in an orange gown attending the Fire and Ice Ball.

"In other news," the newscaster's voice droned, "American Hologram, known as AmHo, has announced that its Vice President, Chris Kappert, and company heiress, Nicholle Ryder, allegedly embezzled twenty billion dollars from the corporation. Arlington County police are investigating…"

Nicholle's body slacked and she collapsed on the couch. A lightheaded consciousness encroached, leaving her disoriented and speechless. Her mind reeled and surreality stole over the scene.

"I don't believe this," she whispered. "It can't be happening."

"Damnit," Chris said. "First your father collapses, then your brother skips town with company cash, Perim's bodyguard kills your friends, and now this. What the hell, Nicholle? We've got to go back to AmHo and clear our names."

When she didn't respond, Chris stalked over, snatched her up by the shoulders, and shook her.

"Nicholle! We have to call Perim and clear this up."

When she regained some semblance of coherency, something tightened in the back of her mind—instincts honed from years past. *From years of covering my ass.*

"Are you insane?" she said. "This Perim wants us out of the way. If we return, he'll just have us arrested. We need to go some place where we can find out more about this guy. Who is he? Where'd he come from? What are his weaknesses? In other words, we need to get the hell out of here."

chapter 4

Wills twisted on the satin sheets, inhaling the salt air that wafted in with the morning light. The woman next to him shifted to her side, surprising him. He had forgotten she was there. The ebony of the sheets blended with her hair, but contrasted with her skin's saffron undertone. The swell of her breasts aroused him, even through his groggy consciousness. He reached over, then a call came through, chiming in his periphery with jarring flashes. *Call from Meloi Ghio.* He swung out of bed and walked out onto the balcony. Closed the glass partition.

His skin tingled with the warmth of Narara Island. A wide expanse of blue ocean lay beyond. He was far away from everything and everyone, and he had wanted to be as far away as possible when the news hit the media.

He answered the cog. "Tell me what's going on."

Meloi held up a glass in a mock toast. He was sitting in an armchair next to a Great Dane. Behind him was a large batik print of a war scene outside the Great Wall.

"Hello to you, too," he said.

"I thought we were past idle chit-chat," Wills said.

"Common courtesy never goes out of style. Now, as to your question… Chris asked Nicholle to take over. She agreed."

Wills turned around, as if Meloi were sitting behind him on the balcony. "What? She hated working there."

"I know. But apparently Chris convinced her. Told me he used the guilt trip about people losing jobs if there's no family continuity."

"Shit. I didn't want her in the picture," Wills said.

"Too late. The company also sold some commercial paper and furniture and fixtures to an upstream supplier to keep the ratios up."

"Predictable. Does she know about Perim?"

Meloi shrugged. "I'm assuming she does by now. He told the whole world that she and Chris embezzeled twenty billion. She's probably on the run now. I'd say he's got the company presidency in sight."

"Shit! I knew I shouldn't have put anything past that bastard."

"You want me to off him?"

Wills paused, stroking his goatee. "No, that would bring more police scrutiny. She can take care of herself. She's been on the street before."

"Yes, me bwana. How go the clinical trials?" Meloi clawed the air with index and middle fingers when he said, "clinical."

"I'm meeting with Rob and Douglas today for an update. I'll let you know."

"All right. Anything else?"

Wills shook his head. "No. Not right now. I'll cog later. Sayo."

Meloi faded to the ocean waves breaking on the shore. The balcony door slid open and the woman whose name Wills hadn't remembered stood in the doorway. The curtains swirled around her bare form.

"I've got an eight thirty conference call," she said in accented English. She raised one eyebrow in a beckoning gesture and approached him. Her hands feathered his muscled torso and a smile caught her lips.

"Bagus sekali," she said.

He didn't know much Indonesian, but he knew that was good. Wills prided himself on keeping in shape. His body was something he could control with absolute certainty, and he paid particular attention to it.

"And I've got a meeting, so we'd better make the most of the next hour." Wills ran his hand down her back, savoring her silky skin. He led her back into the bedroom.

✿

Holographic data screens filled the middle of the room, with numbers scrolling from the top to the bottom of gridless squares. Bodies lined three of the four walls, each on a readout bed. Data hovered—recipient name, donor name, vitals, brain maps, and some other graphics Wills couldn't make out.

He crossed his arms and surveyed the lab with a rare sense of wonder. He silently thanked Thia Wayan. Without the information he'd stolen from her node, none of this would have been possible. And to think he'd just been sniffing around, hoping to find an angle on a foreign client. Instead, he'd stumbled on preliminary studies on consciousness transference.

A few white-coat-clad attendants moved among the patients, adjusting data and dosages.

"Good morning, Mr. Ryder," said a voice behind him.

He twisted around. "Pam. Have you seen Rob and Doug?"

She jerked her head to her left. "They're in the conference room. There's pizza, but you'd better hurry."

"Thanks."

Wills angled past odd-looking machinery and through several holo body scans to make his way to the conference room. He walked in to find the two men poring over data screens.

"Gentlemen," Wills said. "How are things?"

They exchanged a glance, as if each were seeking a confirmation of his own personal assessment.

Rob, the taller of the two, with grey hair and inquisitive eyes, spoke first.

"We're not seeing full personality transference. There's leakage from the original."

"In how many test subjects?" Wills said.

"All of them. Although we get better results in younger subjects," Doug added. "The brain patterning for them is not as fixed as in older ones. And we don't get much use at all out of the brain-damaged burnouts."

Wills had arranged to acquire the bodies of AmHo subscribers who had chosen medinite-assisted suicide—those without concerned friends and family. Instead of the medinites causing death, they put the subject in a coma. He'd greased the palms of a few doctors with questionable qualifications to pronounce death, then leave with the body and ship it to Narara.

"It's not the new Cog 2 server, is it?" Wills said.

"No, the server is fine," Rob said, shaking his head.

"What if you…try stopping the heart, waiting a few minutes, uploading the patterning, then restarting the heart?" Wills said.

"A sort of reboot?" Rob said, skeptically.

"If that's what you want to call it," Wills said. "At this point, I suggest you try everything possible."

Rob backed away from the table and leaned against the glass partition. "It would be better if we started off with a relatively blank slate. Like an adult clone."

Doug looked away. Human cloning was illegal in most countries, although there were tales of rogue labs on floating platforms in international waters that had successfully performed human cloning experiments. Some even said they 'walked among us.' Others said, 'Horseshit.'

"Gentlemen, if clones are what you need, then clones are what you'll get. However, I put the burden on you. You know the rumors. Track them down and get what information you need. My resources are at your disposal. I'm in this for the long haul, but know that neither my time nor my patience is unlimited. So be as quick about it as you can."

"But…" Doug began, then lowered his voice as if in conspiracy. "If you want this to be commercially viable, this will have to be legal in First World countries."

Wills admired the man's business sense. Rare in a scientist, he thought. "You just leave that to me."

"We could also use some more techrus," Rob said. "Some good ones."

"You're in luck," Wills said. "I know just where to get some."

○

Wills slid on his shades after stepping out into the blaze of white sun that reflected off the sand. He walked to the end of the porch and spied a boat in the distance. Watched it trawl across the horizon, waited for the ripples to reach shore. The lab had once been a yacht club for resort-goers. Now it was a holding place for the sick and dying.

He cogged Senator Joan McKay of Maryland. Got her secretary, Mason. She had a high-bridged nose that sloped down to hooked nostrils.

"Mason, is Joan in?"

"Hold on, hon," she said.

Mason blanked out. The next image was that of the senator. She wore a pale green suit that complemented her olive skin and highlighted hair.

"Wills, long time," she said. "Sorry to hear about your father. And what's this about you and your sister absconding with company money?" She leaned back in her chair, intrigue crossing her features.

"It's all a big misunderstanding."

"Mmm hm."

"Everything will be cleaned up next week. Anyway, I have a proposal." He paused.

"Go on."

"This is a long-term proposal. I know this will not happen overnight, but I need you to start research on this legislation."

"Wills, you're teasing me like a burlesque stripper. Out with it."

Wills grinned. "There's the Joan I love and admire. Ready? Human cloning."

She leaned forward, brows knit, and propped her head on one hand. "Are you insane?"

"I can assure you I am not. But…let me take you to dinner when I get back in town. I have some…interesting news to share."

"It had better be fuckin' dynamite," Joan said.

"Don't worry. I'm sure you'll be blown away."

Joan rolled her eyes. "Interface with my schedule and post a date. Ciao."

Wills tapped out and strolled a bit down the beach. The sun, sand, and waves made for a pleasant view. But he wasn't the type to stay long on vacation. He had to be in the middle of things, managing projects, checking financials, running stock numbers, manipulating people and things. That's how he relaxed. Not sitting idly by while the world kept spinning around him. He supposed one day he'd slow down and be content with life. But he figured he wouldn't be disposed to such an existence for another thirty to forty years.

He had worked for his father for the past decade, learning, watching… waiting. Remembering what had happened all those years ago. And now all Wills had to do was wait five days. Five days until he could exact revenge. And it would be sweet, he promised himself.

As for Perim, Wills had installed a setup for him, and he was waiting to see if he took the bait.

chapter 5

"And he's still complaining about not getting secret clearance, bragging that he had it at his last job, and that the managers must be idiots. I mean it's been three years. If he doesn't have it now, he ain't gonna get it. You know what I mean?"

Thia Wayan trained her eyes on Menzel's mouth to help her understand what he was saying. The cacophony in the crowded bar drowned out most conversations, and this was one she had been waiting to hear. Menzel was just an average spotter whose job it was to seek out potential recruits, but Thia had had her eye on a particular recruit for some time. Patience was the name of the game, and it usually paid off in the end.

"Did you invite him here, as I asked?"

"Yeah, but I dunno. He kinda keeps to himself. Said he might drop by, might not. Personally, I think he's a bit stuck up," Menzel said. He kept ogling the brunette at the bar, who returned his interest. Her cleavage threatened to spill out of a tight sweater with a plunging neckline. The sweater kept changing colors, blue, then black, pink, then blue again. Men were so simple, she thought. Thia swirled her gin and tonic, then drained it.

"Well, thank you, Menzel. Your efforts, as always, are appreciated. I think I'll just hang around for a bit, though." She had slipped a five-thousand-dollar money chip under a cardboard coaster when she first sat down. Now she slid the coaster across the table to Menzel.

Menzel's fingers expertly picked up the chip. He winked at her, then headed for the woman at the bar.

Thia retrained her focus on the milling patrons, mentally creating profiles: middle class, average student who used a prominent neighbor's reference to become a senator's aide; Georgetown graduate who's slumming it with her ne'er-do-well boyfriend; administrative assistant who's not shy about using what she has to climb to the next level. It was an exercise designed to keep her mind sharp and relieve boredom. But lately she'd been creating the same few profiles.

Her thoughts were interrupted by a familiar face. Neer Bol.

His hair lay flat, parted to one side, widow's peak pointing down to an aquiline nose. An intelligence still peered from behind his eyes, coldly calculating. A taut Windsor knot lay atop a spread-collar shirt, underneath a dark blue pinstripe suit, sleeves ending in gold cufflinked folds.

He shouldered his way to the bar and raised an arm, trying to get the bartender's attention, who was busy pouring drinks for a group of blondes at the other end. Neer looked out of place with his stiff demeanor and passé fashion, juxtaposed with the three twenty-something males dressed in the latest smoothskins. Colors and images slid over bodies in synchronous timing—proximity patterning.

Thia motioned to the bartender, whom she had tipped generously for her drink, holding up her empty glass and pointing to Neer. The bartender nodded and headed down the bar. He handed Neer his order and, when Neer tried to pay, waved his hand in refusal and tilted his head in Thia's direction. The look on Neer's face almost made her laugh. After he closed his mouth, he eyed her suspiciously, then sidled over to her table. He balanced his drink as he pushed his way through the throng. He edged around the booth and sat down.

"Well, well. Fancy meeting you here," he said. He had the same smooth baritone voice with the slight gravel edge she remembered.

"I just stopped by. Thought this looked like a nice place," Thia said.

"Bull. You're never seen unless you want to be seen. Don't tell me. You've got a spotter at American Hologram."

"You always did cut to the chase." That was one thing about working with those in the business. They knew the routine.

"Did he or she tell you that Kalinska is having money problems, and that Urbana is a closet hetero?" Neer said.

"I'm not interested in the others," Thia said.

"Oh? That so?"

"How long has it been since you worked at the department?"

Out of the window on M Street, white fairy lights illumined the bare trees that lined the sidewalk. Groups of workers passed underneath, on their way to the next bar. The street was a favorite after-work hangout. A recruiter's dream.

Thia turned her attention back at Neer. The vein in his temple throbbed. The mere mention of his old place of employ must have set off internal alarm bells. He swallowed hard.

"Three years, two months, fifteen days."

Three years and the poor bastard still kept track. This should be a cinch. "Ever think of coming back?"

"Every damned day," he said. "But we know that's not happening."

Thia took a drink, then shrugged. "Maybe I can talk to some people."

"Come back as what, your subcontractor? No way. I'd want full reinstatement."

"That might take time. In the meantime—"

"What the hell is it you want, Thia? Just come out with it."

Thia thought over her next move. The job of recruiter was a delicate one, a task to be finessed. Push too hard and a potential spy might bolt; too soft and one wouldn't know what she was talking about. Although she didn't have to worry much about the latter with Neer.

"You're looking handsome as ever, Neer." She smiled as she reached over and ran her finger along the edge of Neer's glass.

Neer threw his head back and laughed out loud. "So that's it. Seduce me and promise my old job back, in return for what—information? How predictable I must be," he said.

Thia suppressed a smirk. Men like Neer might protest, but would jump at the chance to work for intel again. Corporate senior developers no longer had automatic access to top secret information, no opportunity to prepare briefs for high-ranking government officials, no occasional jaunts on Air Force Two. Probably just meetings, corporate propaganda, and production mandates from the higher ups. Not a glamorous prospect.

"Do I at least get dinner first?" he said.

"I know a great place."

○

Thia and Neer walked arm in arm into the restyled Au Pied de Cochon. The aroma of the restaurant's signature dish, emincé de volaille sauce Roquefort, greeted the pair at the door. Dim lighting lent an air of secretive conversation, perfect for the evening's agenda.

"Ah, Mademoiselle Michaud, bienvenu," the host, Michel, said. He stepped forward from the front desk and spoke in a low voice. "Aimeriez-vous la pièce privée?" *Would you like the private room?*

"Oui, Michel. Merci."

Michel reached for two menus and motioned for the pair to follow him. With Neer in tow, she walked past the row of tables populated with Georgetown veterans and decorated with white tablecloths, votive candles, and yellow mums. Michel seated them and left.

Neer studied the dark cherry wood paneling. "Nice place. You have a reserved private room?"

Thia thought the ambient lighting softened Neer's eyes.

"Oh, let's just say it pays to treat staff well." She tapped her foot three times, initiating a continuous sensor sweep that would download the results to her node. A green light flashed in her periphery. The room was clean of bugs. At least the ones she knew about. Technology improved every day. One's enemies—or a neutral party looking to sell information—could be listening in with some new device. It paid to be paranoid.

The waiter entered after knocking and took their orders: the signature dish for both, a bottle of strong wine for dinner, and Green Chartreuse liqueur with dessert to help lower Neer's inhibitions. When the waiter left, Thia kept the conversation light, choosing to wait until dessert to make the offer and close the deal. She hoped Neer was a fast eater.

By the time the crème brûlée arrived, the wine was taking effect, to Thia's satisfaction. She'd managed to maintain her one glass, while Neer had polished off the rest of the bottle, all the while pontificating on his technological prowess.

"He didn't know what the hell he was talking about anyway. He's a finance manager, for cryin' out loud. He barely knew Cog was a trapped ion quantum computer, and he's got the nerve to try to tell me—ME—about decoherence. Ha!"

As her eyes began to glaze over from boredom, she slid closer to Neer, slipped off one of her black leather pumps, and rubbed her foot against his leg. Her fingers brushed the back of his neck, raking through his hair.

With her other hand, she spooned her dessert into her mouth. The savory warmth of the brûlée curled around her tongue. Neer finally stopped talking and looked at her with a wicked grin. Pieces of broccoli stuck in his teeth; green dots crowned his gums. She did her best to ignore it.

His hand shook as he poured the last of the Green Chartreuse into his glass, spilling some onto the white tablecloth. The stain spread, reminding her of a gunshot wound, and she imagined Wills Ryder lying on the floor in front of her, bleeding to death, his life slowly ebbing away. He had stolen information from her, and it had been her ass that had gotten chewed out. She didn't even know he had stolen the secrets until the rumors started. But if she didn't bring him in, there would be hell to pay. *Bastard.*

"You know, you never told me exactly what you wanted," Neer slurred. The cold, sharp intelligence in his eyes had dulled to a hazy obtuseness. She'd seen that look too many times in too many bars, hashhouses, and pakz joints.

"Well, besides Wills Ryder himself, you know more than anyone about Cog, n'est pas?"

"Wills Ryder. Puh! Bastard took the money and ran. Had nothing to do with day-to-day management. And with the old man in a coma and his thieving sister on the run, I predict the company's gonna go down the fema hole." He pointed a shaky finger in Thia's face. "Mark my word."

"Nicholle Ryder, curator at a holographic art museum, acting president of a large corporation, now a suspected felon."

He shrugged. "Yeah, but we got a new VP, Perim Nestor. Maybe the Board will appoint him."

She'd heard Wills had cut and run with a large percentage, but that didn't sound like him. His mantra was power, not money. He was controlling the company from behind the scenes. Somehow.

Neer's face turned down into melancholy anger. "I was one of the best, wasn't I?"

"The best damned research scientist Homeland Intelligence ever had." Thia raised her glass in mock tribute.

"One little mistake," he said. His eyes held a faraway look.

Thia begged to differ with calling an entire career of back-stabbing and insubordination 'one little mistake,' but she nodded her head in agreement. "Bastards don't know what they're missing. But I'm giving you a chance to get back in, if you want it."

"Whaddoo I hafta do?" he slurred.

"There's a rumor that Wills was working on consciousness transference before he left. I just need you to poke around, see if it's on the server. If so, share the wealth."

"Transference of consciousness? Why didn't I hear about it?" Neer said.

"Because you don't have our resources. Do you think Perim or Nicholle knows?"

"If anyone, probably Nicholle. Blood, you know, is thicker than water."

"I see. I don't have to remind you that what's said here is strictly between us," Thia said.

"I'm not an amateur," he protested. His voice was noticeably louder, and Thia knew she would have to close the deal soon, before the management did it for her.

"So, do we have a deal?"

Neer raised his glass, the Green Chartreuse casting a neon glow on his pallid face. "To our deal."

"Excellent. We'll have to work out a system of communication. But we can talk details later."

Neer had a blank look on his face. "Why can't I just send it wiho?"

"I don't trust it."

"Okay, okay. Don't get your panties in a twist." He leaned over and breathed alcohol in her face. "What say we go to your place?" he whispered loudly.

Thia refrained from rolling her eyes and waving her hand in front of her nose. "I'm in the purlieus. Get your coat."

✿

With the advent of fuel cells, people had moved farther out beyond D.C. than before, establishing towns in once-rural areas, now known as the purlieus. The suburbs were abandoned, left to whoever was left—usually the criminal element.

Route 1994 was relatively empty, given that it was a weeknight. Most of the commuters had gone home on the Maglev, and were now ensconced in their cookie-cutter neighborhoods on the edge of nowhere, where pudgy husbands mowed their postage-stamp yards on Saturday mornings. Gossipy housewives walked their children to the park to talk to other moms about the best daycare, or which child had what second-grade teacher. Thia hated the whole scene. But it was the only place she could afford. At the moment, anyway. The rich still inhabited their enclaves in Kensington, Georgetown, and Potomac. The middle class were relegated farther out in the purlieus, while the poor were stuck in rundown isolation in the suburbs.

The high-speed trains had allowed those middle-class earners who wanted the white picket fence to head out to the purlieus in search of good schools, low crime, and convenient shopping. The people had moved beyond the cities, but culture hadn't. Ask a purlieu dweller when the last time was he saw a chamber orchestra and he would look at you as if you had sprouted a second head. Even if the orchestra was, literally, at his fingertips. Tap a finger, et voilà! A string ensemble.

As the car sped past a blurred landscape at 250 miles per hour, Thia lounged in the driver's seat. In her lifetime, auto-pilot reduced the role of the driver to mere observer, and the interior of cars changed accordingly. She tapped up a heated massage and sank into the blanket of hands that stretched under the ostrich skin seat. Fingers kneaded away stress-induced tension.

A low snore emanated from Neer. His mouth hung open as drool leaked from the side. His self-aggrandizing charm had long since dissipated. She figured she would stash him in her bed until morning, tell him how great he was, then send him on his way.

A blue light flashed three times in her periphery. Her corporate handler. He wanted an update. She tapped out the menu and wrote a message summarizing the night's events. He would be happy to find out Neer had taken the bait. When the message encrypted, she sent it along. She felt more confident sending messages since they had built additional quantum repeater stations, but she preferred the dead drop approach, which she still used with her own informants. Or maybe she just liked the subterfuge. Skulking around in the bushes was more palpable than tapping a finger. But if she added another country to her list of employers, it'd be hard to keep track.

To pacify her Chinese handler, she would have to make a stop.

The car passed the service station where her own dead drop was, but she had to make sure she wasn't being followed. Thia turned off at the second exit past the station and meandered through darkened neighborhoods with her lights off as she prepared the message for Wu Ji.

Convinced no one was tailing her, Thia ordered the car back onto the highway, heading for the service station. Neer still slept peacefully. *Must be getting old, Neer.*

At the station, she exited the car and opened the back door. She grabbed a stiff leash and activated the diode. A small white terrier appeared at the end of the leash, eagerly sniffing out its surroundings. She took the dog toward the wooded area in back of the service station.

She walked about a quarter mile along a dirt path that led to denser underbrush, until it faded into brambles. The bare trees provided less cover and she decided it would be her last drop at this location. One of the telegraph poles along the old service road might do.

A decaying bench sat off to the right, half hidden under brush. Several of its slats were missing and the scrolled iron edges had rusted. Thia surveyed her surroundings, then leaned over and loosened the arm of the bench, pulling it to one side. The dog sat and panted. She slid the message into a small hole. The Chinese, too, would be pleased to hear she was in a position to receive information on their shopping list. And she knew there would be a package waiting for her the next night.

She stood up and sneezed. The spores from the evergreens always got to her this time of year. As her head bent, the hairs on the back of her neck stood on end as a searing heat rushed past her.

Pulse weapon!

She dropped to the ground, falling through the white terrier, who barked in protest. Thia squeezed her hand underneath her, drawing her weapon from her inside pocket. Her mind raced. *Who could have known?* Did Neer betray her that quickly? She doubted it. He might be an arrogant SOB, but not a snitch. Wu Ji looking for direct access to her sources? Make himself look good for the Ministry of Security? Anything was possible.

Another shot pulsed and she caught the direction. Two o'clock. Scrambling to her knees, she fired three wide-dispersal shots blindly into the dark woods, sizzling the air, then dropped to the ground. No return fire. Two more shots seared over her, this time from behind.

Fema!

There was another shooter. The dog growled in reply. She deactivated the leash and the dog faded into nonexistence. Thia crawled in the direction of the car. The thorny underbrush scratched her face and caught her hair. A hundred pinpricks needled her skin through her sweater as she pressed forward.

Something rustled behind her and she wheeled her arm around and fired twice. Blue flare cauterized the air, setting the top of the underbrush on fire.

"Aaaah!"

Then silence. Thia waited in the underbrush, straining to hear movement. Her heart pounded in her ears. Pain welled up in her muscles as she tensed and she forced herself to relax and control her breathing. *Breathe, breathe.* Panic was of no use.

She had to find out who was firing at her, which faction. Corporate? Chinese? Pissing off clients was something she tried to avoid, although at times it couldn't be helped. Intelligence agencies were usually cautious when dealing with free agents. Provoking an agency into issuing a hit was just one mistake away.

The shooter behind her was probably dead, but she'd have to check. She crawled backward, slowly, still listening for movement, until her foot felt something hard. A boot. She twisted around and fired. Burnt flesh. A large red hole that curled black at the edge filled the man's chest. The nauseating smell of cooked bowels bloomed up.

She kept crawling backward, training her gun on the unmoving form. Her toe tapped his plasma gun. She jerked her toe away, fearful of searing off her leg. She picked up his gun and checked the chamber. Enough energy for five more shots. Her own gun had seven. She crawled back farther, until the dead man's face came into view.

Kirill Genechko. A low-level mercenary. Ukrainian. The kind government agencies hired to do their dirty work. Or at least the agencies that hadn't much experience in wetware, the agencies not involved in intel, like the Department of Agriculture.

Thia crouched low and struggled to prop up the dead man. He had to weigh at least two-fifty and she had to strain not to grunt in exertion.

Another shot scorched past, frying the man's head, missing hers by inches. She let go and the man fell on her arm as she toppled over, face up. One more blast flew over her, burning her nose.

I must be hot on someone's ass for them to try this. She slid her arm out from under his lambskin coat. *They must pay well, whoever they are.*

Deciding she couldn't wait in the bushes forever, she readied the two guns and crouched. She stood and ran in a zigzag pattern back down the dirt path, toward the station. She had to get Neer to a safe location.

Shards of blue pulsed past her, searing her coat. Four o'clock. She leveled her weapons and squeezed off several shots. Two shots answered back, one slicing her shoulder. She bit her lip through the pain and ran, firing behind her until she ran out of shots, then reached the edge of the woods. A vision of her car loomed up. She fell to the ground, shocked.

Neer sat in the passenger's seat, half his face gone. Burnt black, along with the door. Thia rolled left, behind a large garbage bin. More pulses fired. The station was deserted, patrons no doubt scared off by the gunfire. Footsteps. The gunman approached.

There!

A car sat idling, a beige Reno. One of the cheap imports from Kenya, but any port in a storm. She dashed for the open passenger-side door and slammed it shut behind her, keeping low as she slid in the driver's seat. Hunching to the side, she engaged the reverse gear and screeched backward, then tore out of the parking lot as blue pulses slashed the air around her. She reached I-1994 and pushed the car to its 300 mph limit. Streetlights blurred past.

She couldn't even work out the identity of the second gunman, but he was definitely a pro. She had been stripped of her car and her source. A first. There had been more than one and they knew where she was going. The information Neer had access to must've posed a danger to someone. The question was, who? There was one place to start looking. Nicholle Ryder.

chapter 6

Nicholle snatched a bag out of the closet and headed for the transport tube.

"Where are we going?" Chris said.

"Away from here. I don't have any plans written in stone at the moment. We'll make it up as we go."

"As we go?"

They stepped out of the tube and Nicholle jogged to the back of the parking lot. Chris kept up.

"Look, unless you happen to have access to a safe house, I'd suggest you hush."

She stopped at a small black car and pressed her thumb on the lock. It glowed green and she yanked the door open.

"Manual doors?" Chris said.

"Get the fuck in."

Chris slid into the seat, his face drawn up in wariness. Nicholle started the car and eased out of the lot.

"With tinted windows, no one should be able to see us. And the car is registered in a foreign diplomat's name."

"How'd you manage that?"

"Couple of friends. Check the news, see what's going on," Nicholle said.

Chris searched on their names and transferred the images to the car's diodes. Scrolling text appeared on the passenger side of the windshield:

Nicholle Ryder of American Hologram took a page from her brother's book. She has been accused of embezzling twenty billion dollars from the company. Her brother, William, was accused of taking fifty billion earlier today, after their father, Geren, was rushed to a hospital when he collapsed at work. Perim Nestor, American

Hologram's vice president, reported the money missing this evening. Police have put out an APB for her.

"That bastard! And I haven't even met him! We can't go back. We can't even call the police. Come to think of it, I'm afraid to call my friends. The ones I have left. The police might have them tapped."

"I've got a friend I can call," Chris said. "He'll let us stay for a while."

✿

Dried Earth Boulevard, Wind Rider Way, Burnt Mountain Path—names of streets in Columbia. Like disjointed, random sentences in a pakz-induced haze. Nicholle had heard tell Columbia was a city with premier neighborhoods once upon a time, with tree-lined streets and emerald grass. Now it boasted a run-down mall, dilapidated housing, and dirt-filled front yards decorated with rusted cars.

She and Chris drove through the neighborhoods, passing house after house with peeling paint and broken shutters.

"Nice place," she deadpanned.

"Not everyone's an heiress," Chris said.

She bit down a retort.

"Left here," he said.

She turned on Canyonhead Lane, onto a cracked asphalt street, where trash littered the gutters and cats' eyes peered from sewers.

"What's the address?" she said.

"Here it is. On the right."

She pulled into the driveway. Nicholle shook as she alighted from the driver's side. Since the shooting, she had put up a front, but now she was crashing. Her legs quavered as she staggered to the front of the car and leaned against the hood. Her heart thumped in her chest, banging in her ears. Chris walked around and put his hand on her shoulder.

"Hey, you okay?" he said.

"Just shaken. Guess it's been longer than I thought since I got shot at. Not quite used to it."

"Well, c'mon. Let's go in." Chris motioned his head toward the house, a narrow blue frame affair with dead grass in the front lawn and a leaning Bradford pear tree. The style reminded Nicholle of the pictures she had seen of her great-grandmother's house back in the late 1900s.

"This one's your friend's?"

"Yeah, Corland. Taught me everything I know about wiho mesh," Chris said.

"I thought you were Geneware certified."

"I am. But that's front door. Corland knows the back door, side door, trap door."

"Ah. Mm, they still have concrete." Nicholle noticed the cracks in the driveway and sidewalk. Chris cut her a look, and she raised a hand. "I won't be a snob. Promise."

When they reached the top of the stairs, a bell sounded from inside the door. Beethoven's *Fifth*.

A far-away clanking sounded, then grew louder, coming up the street. A red truck sporting flashing yellow and blue lights hovered up the street, then pulled into the driveway, sounding as if it would fall out of midair. Shaking violently, it barely cleared the mailbox, then landed with a loud bang.

The door whisked open and a bald-headed man with heavy brows arched over dark eyes emerged. He wore a black viscous sleeveless shirt that varied its texture continuously, but whose sensors were painfully obvious under the shifting material. The man smiled generously when he spied Chris.

"Chris! You nuch. Long time no see."

They hugged like old friends while Nicholle visually scanned the man for weapons.

"Hey, man, it's been a while," Chris said. "Hey, this is Nicholle Ryder. Nicholle, this is L.G."

L.G. reached out a hand. Nicholle nodded as she shook it. "Just call me Nick," she said, slipping into her old persona.

Chris threw her a look, but she shook her head.

"So what brings you here? I heard you landed some mahatma job at AmHo. Didn't think we'd see you again," L.G. said.

L.G. walked inside and Chris and Nicholle followed close behind. The hardwood foyer opened to a long hallway with a staircase to the left. Grunge yellow covered the walls, accented with brown marks and small holes. Old-style computers blanketed in a layer of dust crowded the hallway, forcing the pair to walk single file back to the kitchen. Nicholle stepped gingerly along the creaking floor, wondering if it would give way any minute.

The kitchen lay ahead, mirroring the grunge yellow of the hallway. A microgen oven sat on a burgundy counter littered with dirty dishes. A netfridge stood to the right, displaying its contents onscreen: two cases of beer, an apple, and an expired bottle of French dressing.

Nicholle forced her face into a mask of tight indifference, even as she longed to call for a biohazard unit.

"You guys want a beer?" L.G. said.

"No, I'm not thirsty," Chris said. He turned. "Nick?" His voice dripped sarcasm.

"No, thanks, though," she replied.

"Cor's downstairs," L.G. said.

"Great," Chris said.

Chris opened the door to the basement and started down the stairs with Nicholle in tow. She had expected a dank-looking room with more cracked concrete and perhaps some exposed wires. Instead, the floor was blanketed with rich brown carpet, offset by beige walls decorated with murals of oils by the masters that shifted one to the next: *La Primavera* by Botticelli, *Daniel in the Lions' Den* by Rubens, *The Astronomer* by Vermeer. They changed in rhythm to pulsating music that sounded throughout the basement.

A flash of red drew her attention away from the murals toward the middle of the large room. A huge red dragon with two fire-breathing heads clawed at a knight. The knight wielded a broadsword, stabbing the air as it kept missing the weaving dragon's head. The sword finally found its target and slashed down on one of the dragon's necks. The head fell off, hemorrhaging blood onto the carpet. The other head spewed a stream of fire at the knight, who raised his shield in defense, letting the fire wash over him. When the dragon's attack relented, the knight reared up and threw the broadsword at the dragon. Its tail whipped around and batted away the sword, which disappeared at the edge of the carpet. The music grew louder. The dragon leaped forward and landed on the knight, knocking him to the floor, then raised its head with a plangent roar. As the echoes of the roar faded, the music crescendoed and the dragon's head dove for the knight.

"No!" Nicholle cried. She was embarrassed as soon as she uttered the word, forgetting for that split second that the scene was not real.

The dragon froze, the music stopped, and the knight's armor faded away to reveal a brown-skinned man with hooded eyes and shoulder-length cornrows.

"Cor. Hey, man," Chris said. He helped the knight up. Two people's voices could be heard from one of the back rooms, whose door was ajar. They sounded as if they were arguing.

"Hey, keep it down back there! Jeeb, Chris," Cor said. "Look at you. All suited up and shit." He looked past Chris to Nicholle and smiled. He snapped his finger and the music stopped.

"Nicholle Ryder, daughter of Geren Ryder, who invented wireless hologram," Cor said. "On the run from the cops."

"Sheesh, news travels," Nicholle said, slightly taken aback. "But I never stole any money."

She changed the subject, gestured toward the murals. "You like art? Interesting choice of paintings in the rotation. Any particular reason?"

Cor snorted. "That was left here by the previous owner."

"Oh. Well, anyway…thanks for letting us in."

"Chris here just said you needed a place to stay for a few nights. There's an extra room on the second floor where you two can stay. Just share groceries and utilities, at least for now. Any long-term stay will have to be negotiated," Cor said.

"Oh, we're not—" she began.

"Thanks, Cor. We really do appreciate this." He emphasized the word 'appreciate' and raised an eyebrow in Nicholle's direction. The two voices in the back got louder.

"…been listening? Oron himself decanonized the animated version before he died. It doesn't—"

"Oron can't decanonize because he didn't own the rights. What are you, deaf and dumb?"

"He's the creator of Colony. His word is law."

"He's dead. The production company gets to decide canon."

"Those idiots? The prequels sucked."

"Will you two keep it down?" Cor said. The fighting ceased, replaced by various blips and bleeps from a gaming program.

"They go through that every week," Cor said.

"What are they arguing over?" Nicholle said.

"The show, Colony," Chris said.

"I've heard of that. But isn't it about thirty years old?"

"It began thirty years ago, but there's been so many incarnations, it's hard to keep track. Some people want to accept everything as part of the Colony universe, others only what they like. It's been the subject of many lively debates," Chris said.

"Hm." She didn't quite get the point of the argument. *To each his own.* "Oh, while it's on my mind, let me pay you for some groceries." She remembered the netfridge display, decided she wouldn't survive long on beer and salad dressing, and wondered if they delivered groceries to this part of town.

"Do they deliver here?"

"Yeah, but you hafta go down to the corner to get it," Cor said.

Nicholle tapped open a menu. She'd transfer five thousand for the time being. A list of banks glowed down the right-hand side. She picked the National Bank of Kenya.

Zero balance.

"What?" she said.

"What's wrong?" Chris said.

"Uh, nothing. Probably a glitch." Perhaps the museum had been late in sending out the payroll, or perhaps Riklo had put in her Family Leave as a separation. She tried again to request a balance but the result was the same. Then she tried to access Zurich Nationale. Zero.

Heat bloomed her face and traveled down her neck. It couldn't be. *What if*—? She accessed the savings account. Zero. The mutual fund account. Zero. Her fingers blurred in motion as she tapped out the various sequences to access the accounts—Swiss numbered account, fictitiously named account, wingspread investment accounts, IRA, overnight repurchases. All zero. Her stocks were still there, but no bank would lend her money against those. She was flat broke.

Her mouth dried, a hard stickiness that cleaved her lips to her teeth. Her legs weakened and buckled. She would've fallen to the floor if Chris hadn't caught her up by the arm.

"Hey, you okay?" he said.

She said nothing. The last time she'd gone broke, it had driven her back to her brother, forced her to grovel. And she vowed she'd never again be in a position to beg him, or anyone, for help. Chris helped her over to the couch and sat beside her.

"Nicholle. Talk to me."

"Hey, she OD?" Cor said.

"No," Chris said. "I don't know what's the matter."

"There's a free clinic down the road."

"Thanks. I think she'll be okay. Nicholle." Chris tapped her cheek with his hand. "Nicholle."

"I'll leave you two alone," Cor said. "And go tell these guys what canon really is."

"Knock yourself out," Chris said.

Even when she was on the street, her father had diverted her accounts, but left some money there. A fallback. *A crutch.* But what would she do now? The only thing she had left was stock. And she couldn't sell it to anyone except her father or brother.

"I'm broke," she said.

"You're what?"

"I'm broke." It had been kind of him to bring her here, in spite of everything. He could have abandoned her, told her she was on her own, instead of risking his own life to help her. He at least deserved the truth.

"What are you talking about? You're rich. You have money."

"Not anymore. All my accounts have a zero balance. Perim, I'm guessing, wiped them clean."

"Are you sure? I mean you accessed the right—"

"Of course I'm sure. I can't even afford a fleabag motel." She fell back onto the couch, sinking into the plastimold, sinking into the surrealness that was her life.

"I'll check my accounts."

"Good luck," she said, sarcastically.

He tapped, punched, scrolled, and poked, but he kept repeating curse words, which told Nicholle that Perim had cleaned him out, too.

"He's good, this Perim. Did I tell you he was my brother?"

Chris looked at her as if she had sprouted another head.

"It's true. The family lawyer told me. Apparently, my father had an affair decades ago. My father just found out this week Perim was his. Probably why he made him vice president. But I'm wondering if my father knew about Perim all along and just didn't want to deal with it. He never really was good at family."

"Nicholle."

"And now we're both broke. I mean, I have about fifty thousand in cash in my bag, but how long will that last?"

"Nicholle, we've got four hackers in this house. We can back door Cog and find out where your money is. Or at least get back some of it."

Nicholle sat up. "You serious?"

"I'm sure Perim changed the security protocols, but I know the system administrator rules for the wall, the algorithms for ciphers, and of course, I left several back doors to Cog." He assumed a self-satisfied look.

"I knew I brought you along for a reason."

Chris took her hand in his and squeezed. "It's been a rough night. You okay?"

"I've been chased by a killer, had my friends killed, was framed, and was robbed blind by my own vice president. It was easier on the street. When I was with Tuma, as least I knew where I stood."

"Wait right here."

Chris released her hand and headed to the room in the back. He knocked on the door. "Challenge," he said. The door flew open and the anxious face of Cor appeared, a wide grin on his face.

"Seriously?" Cor said.

"Yeah, get your ass out here, nuch," Chris said.

Cor and the two people who had been arguing over Colony scrambled out of the room. "Nicholle, this is Arn and his girlfriend, Trenar," Chris said.

"Jeeb," she said, repeating the greetings she'd heard earlier.

Trenar sported long bright red hair and heavy eye shadow that matched her pink miniskirt. Arn's hair matched hers in length, only his was jet black. His eyes were deep brown with red veins radiating from the pupil, as if he'd been up all night.

"So what's going on?" Arn said.

"Nicholle's and my accounts were wiped clean by an AmHo VP. We have to either find a way to get our funds back, or embezzle some from the company," Chris said.

Arn whistled. "Ain't gonna be easy. Oh, but you know the codes, right Chris?"

"I know the codes, but I'm sure they've been changed. And they've got military-quality sentinels. Although the death spike's been neutralized."

"Well let's batter up and see what we can see," Cor said.

"Nicholle's with me, mesh baby TA," Chris said.

Chris, Cor, Arn, and Trenar reached for their fryers and pulled them down over their heads. They were supposed to provide added focus of synaptic activity and protection against transmitted viruses. Chris handed one to Nicholle, who eyed it suspiciously. She had never worn one before, mostly out of fear. Rumors of fried brains.

"Go on, it's safe. They've improved since the first generation." Chris winked at her.

She stuck the fryer on her head and waited. The others gathered around in a circle, calling up menus in the midst of them, visible to the others. Chris guided her to a position in back of and slightly to the left of him.

"Follow my movements and try to keep up. If you can't, just poke around and see what you can find. Sometimes dumb luck happens in a sortie."

Nicholle nodded and called up her menu, the source code displayed on the right-hand side.

"We'll each try a different node on the grid. Chris, security, Arn, accounting, Trenar, human resources, I'll take R and D. And on my mark. Mark," Cor said.

Fingers raced in mid-air, moving over lightup commands as they activated and inserted programs and blackholes, drawing the sentinels in toward them and away from the inserted programs. Nicholle had seen Chris do it on more than a few occasions, and although she knew the strategy, she didn't have much idea as to its execution.

On each menu, the blackholes wound in a spiral, imprinting black curlicues on the source code. Sentinels rushed to the code, their tails trying to sweep away the invaders. Hidden programs burrowed behind protocols, trying to find weaknesses, an unshielded transom, anything that would allow itself to become part of the system.

Nicholle tried hard to keep up with Chris, but it was impossible for her to mirror his movements. He was too fast. The others were fast, as well, calling up and discarding systems in the time it took for the brain to register a stubbed toe.

She decided to hang back and search around where she was, namely the main node. A story popped up, even as the purple specks filtered down.

Perim Nestor, vice president of American Hologram, spoke on today's events. "All cogs to Nicholle Ryder's node have gone unanswered," he said. "It's a shame that she stole from the very employees and subscribers who have kept her in business all these years."

Mr. Nestor also said that Ms. Ryder dropped out of the social scene last year when she became addicted to illegal substances. He alleged she had become involved with a drug dealer named Tuma, who was twice convicted for drug trafficking.

After living on the streets for several months, Ms. Ryder returned to her family. She subsequently entered Bright Horizons Rehabilitation Center and completed the program. "If you're reading this, Nicholle, we just want you back. Just return the money, and no charges will be filed against you."

Her secret was out—all the way. She had been able to lie about her disappearance to colleagues—an extended vacation in Europe—but no longer.

She checked the news sites, but they hadn't picked up the story. As soon as they could corroborate Perim's account, no doubt they would.

"Got a moron here," Cor said. "Going to try and break in."

"Could be a trap," Arn said.

"Roger that," Cor replied.

Cor pushed aside algorithmic code like a breast-stroke Olympian. Deeper into the core, until they could all see the pink and black of the central system. Chris rode his tail, covering any aftershocks of their intrusion. It was easy going so far.

"Too easy," Chris said.

At that utterance, a bright red flash pierced the blue mesh, directly behind the node Chris had just passed. He didn't see it, careening forward after Cor.

"Chris!" Nicholle shouted.

The blackholes began winding backward, hidden programs suddenly blinking in neon reds and pinks. Sentinels swooped down in swarms, their tails sweeping clean the tampered nodes.

"Shit, it was a trap. He was waiting for me. Regroup!" Chris said.

Arn, Trenar, and Cor dropped a shield in front of them and spiraled out, spinning like tornadoes, zigzagging around sentinels.

Chris's arms flailed. His knees buckled, sending him pitching and yawing. Nicholle stepped forward and caught him as he fell. They both dropped to the floor. His dead weight pinned her.

She took off her fryer as hot sweat covered her body and a gnawing pain in her head curled around the edge of her mind. She rolled Chris off her, praying he was all right. The pain became more insistent, tightening around her eyes. It corkscrewed toward the middle of her skull, and she rolled over in agony. She cradled her head, willing the pain to go away.

Cor, Trenar, and Arn writhed on the floor, in seemingly as much pain as she. She crawled over to Chris and reached through the wretched throbbing to remove his fryer and toss it aside. She clawed his shoulders and shook.

"Chris, wake up!"

He lay limp, flopping about at her insistent shaking. The pangs spiked behind her eyes. "Chris!"

She looked at the others. Trenar made it to a standing position and began staggering around the room, bumping into furniture. Tears mingled with mascara and eye shadow and they ran down her face in clown-like anguish.

Cor and Arn each managed a lopsided crawl as they cradled their head with one hand. A spasm bent around Nicholle's neck and spine, sending her flat on her back. Her head sank into Chris's stomach. But instead of being moved by the rhythmic up-and-down motion of his breathing, she remained still, his stomach stiff and unyielding. The realization hit her slowly, through the murkiness of incomprehension.

"He's not breathing!" she screamed.

The pain spiked one last time. Darkness descended.

chapter 7

Brilliant yellow leaves gleamed in the tall oaks of Parklawn Cemetery. The massive trees stood guard over their charges. A soaring rustling danced in the upper branches, drowning the sound of traffic on Viers Mill Road. Perim lifted his face and breathed in the fall air. The smell of a fire wafted by, bringing with it the memories of the fireplace in the small efficiency apartment he and his mother had shared nearby. During the weeks they couldn't afford heat, they lit a fire in a small covered fire pit, sometimes cooking noodles and hot dogs in a pot.

Those were the times he liked best—even when there was little to eat—because it was just his mom and him. No men were there to threaten him or make his mother scream in the night. Then the food got too scarce and his mother would go out at nights, coming home early in the morning, but bringing delicious meat, fruit, cheese, and even cookies and popsicles. Then his mother would feel guilty, as she had said, and would stay home nights, studying for classes she took during the day. He didn't know what she meant by feeling guilty, until he was in sixth grade. Then he had figured it out.

But when she did attend class, he would sometimes sit with her, bored with Napoleon and Erasmus, but fascinated with supply and demand and the accounting equation. He would take notes himself in those classes, even filling in what his mother had missed. On various occasions, the professor would call on him and he would answer correctly. He had liked that. But his mother liked history, not business, so he was disappointed when she changed her major. He had been looking forward to learning more about intrinsic stakeholder commitment.

He kneeled by her headstone and placed a bouquet of white roses in the holder.

"Hey, Ma. Nice day, eh? The leaves, they're practically glowing. Must've had a lot of rain this summer. Not that I remember.

"I found Dad, from the information you told me just before you passed. I have a brother and a sister, too. William. They call him Wills. And Nicholle. He's an ass, but haven't met her yet. But you know they'll have to go. And then I'll take down the company. And you can rest in peace."

With Nicholle out of the way, he'd be able to do as he pleased. As Geren's son, the board would most likely vote him as president, and then he would have accomplished what he set out to do. He could use the embezzlement as an excuse to start laying off employees and selling off assets. He'd pocket as much as he could before the company went under. He chuckled. Whoever wanted it could buy it at a fire-sale price. *Now that will be sweet revenge.*

He headed back to the office.

✿

Perim looked down the length of the table at the Board of Directors. The board room of American Hologram boasted a twenty-foot mahogany table, a Persian rug, and an art deco ice bucket once owned by Coco Chanel. The AmHo logo beamed in the circular window as light shone through it, a world globe flanked by two yellow half-circle arrows. Written within: Universal Service.

What a crock. Perim thought the logo a product of Geren's ego. And it would soon be gone.

"Members of the board. I've called this emergency meeting to make an announcement. And I'll cut to the chase. I am the illegitimate son of Geren Ryder."

He paused for reaction. Everyone looked up, some with slacked jaws, some with wide eyes, some with both. He continued.

"As you can see from the document I'm forwarding to your nodes, Geren planned to put me on a six-month trial, then insert me in the line of succession behind William and Nicholle. However, since they have not only shirked their duties to this company, but engaged in criminal activity, I respectfully ask that the Board make me acting president so that I can help tamp down this PR nightmare we've been going through."

"How do we know for sure that you're his son?"

The question came from Jerry Maven, head of Solixna Pharmaceuticals.

Perim forced a smile. "I am also forwarding…" He scrolled the air with his finger and selected two documents. Forwarded. "…DNA test results, my resume, and a description of the firm I, until recently, was president of. I am a qualified candidate. And since I don't want to take up more of your time than is necessary, I will leave the room, and you can put it to a vote."

✿

Perim waited in his office while the Board voted. He swiveled in his chair, ruminating on how to draw down the accounts. He'd need a lackey, someone naïve, or close to it. Naïveté was a rare commodity these days.

Vedor Smith. It came to him almost instantly.

He cogged Vedor.

Vedor invariably garnered pity with his five-foot two-inch frame and a beard that faded into prepubescent skin in some spots. To make himself look older, he always wore suits, or at least Perim surmised that was the reason. Most techrus looked as if they had just crawled out of the sewer.

Vedor was beaming. Perim had never seen anyone so happy to be at work. If only all his employees were like that, turnover would be nonexistent. Too bad human cloning was outlawed. He could make a killing by selling loyal, enthusiastic employees to companies around the world.

"Since the recent breach in security regarding bank accounts, I've set up new accounts in the satellite banking system. They'll receive a lot of wi-cash transfers. And because the amounts are above the insured limit for a bank, I need to move the monies around, split them up. Okay? I have a schedule that I'll send you. I need for you to set it up."

"No problem. Just give me the list of banks and amounts to transfer."

"That's the thing. The list will change every day, so I'll be sending new ones. Could even be several times a day."

"Right. I'll take care of it."

Either he didn't know about laundering money or he was stringing Perim along. But Vedor didn't seem the type to know about such things. Not that appearances couldn't be deceiving, he just had an innocence that was hard to feign. From the shiny new shoes to the neatly combed hair, Vedor radiated naïveté. No furtive glances to see whether Perim believed his last words, no quick movements when surprised. Still… something niggled in the back of Perim's mind. It was probably his paranoia.

"Oh! I wanted to show you where I dubbed up the grid." Vedor transferred a holoimage to Perim. A blue grid of dense mesh glimmered in the dimmed light. Pink nodules shone in a pattern on the blue mesh, each radiating lines that extended to the edge.

"We had an attempted intrusion last night, but security held."

"Really? Can you send me the feed?"

"Sure. Okay, I've laid an error correction mesh to cut down on polarization fluctuations and double photon emissions. Makes the server more secure and helps eliminate batter attempts."

"I'm impressed, Vedor. Excellent. Only this nodule in the bottom corner, it doesn't shine as brightly as the others."

"Oh, that's probably just an anomaly in the laser diodes."

Was that a moment's hesitation?

"I see. Well, as I said, excellent work. And now, I've got another meeting to attend, so if you don't mind." Perim rose and Vedor jumped out of his seat.

"Of course. I'll be in my office if you need me." Vedor walked to the door, beaming a smile back at Perim as he went.

Perim tapped his chin and gave instructions to Cog. "Activate the tap in Vedor's office."

Was Vedor a spy? He would know one way or another soon.

He tapped open a line to the communication vice president, Liz Bryn. Her slender brown face held a look of deep concern.

"What's wrong, Liz?"

"The news of scandal filtered through our S&P rating. It took a dive, and wireheads are pinging me left and right, 'specially the *Banner*. It's all, 'Gather 'round, boys, and bring a rope while you're at it.'"

"Liz, you're all doom and gloom. This will blow over, mark my words." Liz had a tendency for melodrama, which usually made for a good communications/propaganda officer in the staid world of wiho providers, but Perim wondered if it would be a liability in a time of scandal.

"I'd rather be marking the days off my ski vacation in the Alps, but it looks like I'll be chained to my desk for the time being. Any marching orders?"

"Make nice, like with the mainstream media. Just tell them we cannot comment on an ongoing investigation, but that the alleged charges have been committed by those who have already left the company. Our financial position is strong and we're sure that American Hologram will be exonerated."

"Standard shmeck. Look, they've already started digging, so it'll only be a matter of time. I hope you've got a Plan B."

"Don't worry, Liz. I definitely have a plan."

chapter 8

The odor in the small motel lobby reminded Thia of the moldy shed at her grandmother's house, where she was sent to retrieve various gardening tools when she was a child. She had been afraid of the dark, dank lean-to, but even more afraid of her grandmother.

The motel lobby held two stained chairs that formed a half square in the middle of the floor. The worn rug looked as if it hadn't been vacuumed in a year. Clashing curtains topped with a layer of dust shielded the musty room from the glare of the neon sign outside. One bright light shone above the registration counter, casting gloomy shadows over the rest of the small lobby. A grinning jack-o'-lantern that sat next to an outmoded computer monitor greeted her from the edge of the counter.

"Can I help you?" The speaker was a burly man with terracotta skin and wispy hair. Either he couldn't afford hair replacement therapy or he didn't care that the top of his head looked like a moth-eaten mohair sweater.

"I'd like a room for the night. Smoking," Thia said.

"No problem." A tag bearing the name, Shiloham Zyan, was affixed to his shirt. "Where you from?" He flashed a bright smile as he began tapping on the monitor screen.

"North Carolina," Thia replied. Which was true. A little truth went a long way in keeping aliases straight. She scanned him and sent the visual feed to the central imaging lab. The quick and dirty search yielded preliminary information, scrolling in orange on the edge of her vision: Shiloham Zyan was the owner/operator of a small motel on Route 301, born in Augusta, Georgia, married with five children, whose electronic transmissions showed no criminal activity. He was having an affair with a Ravi Benar from Odenton, looked at porn sites two to three times a week, and had a recent prostate infection, most likely caused by a prior case of chlamydia.

"Ah, I have a friend from North Carolina. How was the traffic coming up?"

"There was an accident on ninety-five, so I cut over to three-oh-one down by Richmond. Figured I could take ninety-seven up to Baltimore." People became suspicious of those who refused to engage in small talk, so it was a skill Thia learned early on. The more details offered, the more believable the story.

"Oh, yes. Baltimore is just up the road."

"Yeah, well, I was just about to fall asleep, so I figured I'd best stay the night somewhere. Better safe than sorry."

"Oh, no question. Okay, just give me your national ID card, please, and sign the screen." He turned the monitor toward her, proffering a stylus.

Thia did as she was bidden.

"Okie dokie. I have you in room number seven."

"Ah, my lucky number."

Shiloham grinned. "Mine, too." He winked at Thia, who did her best to maintain her composure as she took the key card. He had some nerve, she thought. The door banged shut as she left the rancid lobby.

The pungent tang of stale sweat accosted her as she entered her room. She tossed her travel bag on the bed, then went to each window and opened it. A small ceiling fan hung over the bed and she turned it on full blast.

The modest room held a bed, a nightstand, and a dresser that looked as if it might fall in on itself. The bathroom boasted a toilet and a sonic cleaner so tiny she would have to kneel inside it. What were motels coming to now? In a few more years, guests would probably have to stay in coffin-sized rooms. They were already being offered at airports for those who missed their flights, or were snowed in.

Thia didn't turn on the lights, but let her eyes grow accustomed to the dark. She sat on the bed and spiraled into Cog. Needles of color—red, purple, chartreuse—shot away from her, then coalesced into a helical whorl.

"Welcome to Cognition," sounded in her head. She grabbed a pack of cigarettes from her bag, lit one, and sat down on the bed. Smoke spiraled and hung in the dark room within the translucent red menu. She took a drag and blew the spiral into an aura.

Nicholle hung out with the jet set, sometimes reported on in the society pages, usually seen with some designer or her man of the month. She seemed to change mates like she changed hairstyles. *Like her brother.*

Thia didn't have to look far. The front recto of the *Ynquirer* featured a dazzling picture of Nicholle in a red beaded evening gown, leaving the Kennedy Center. Stock photo, had to be. She was at least ten pounds heavier the last time Thia saw her. The headlines blared the news: A Family Affair! Company President Makes Off With $20 B! Brother Made Off With $50 B!

Thia scanned the article and found Nicholle had eluded the authorities, that the company techru was missing, and that she was once linked with the Quatrocellini heir, Marc.

"I remember him," Thia said to herself.

So Nicholle was on the run, most likely with Chris Kappert, and not likely to turn up at any of her residences, knowing the boys in blue would be hounding her. Which meant she had gone underground. Thia tried to imagine Nicholle living anywhere that didn't have golden faucets and fawning servants. She was probably driving Kappert crazy, poor guy.

But where were they? They could be anywhere, in some rundown building in the suburbs, a basement in the purlieus, a downtown apartment. If she could track Nicholle's financial transactions, it would make it a hell of a lot easier. Thia punched up the DOI database and entered Nicholle's name. The recto flooded with information, psychological profile—ENFP; employer—National Gallery of Art; places frequented—work, restaurants, designer stores, friends' houses; bank, credit, investment accounts—zero balances. *Zero balances? What the—?*

She must have drawn down her accounts. Maybe Kappert had transferred the money for her. If so, she was planning on staying underground for a while. Which meant Thia had better find her before she got good at it. She leaned back and stubbed out her cigarette in the ashtray on the nightstand, then settled in for a long night of searching.

After a greasy hamburger and four hours of trawling through call records and security camera feeds at Nicholle's favorite haunts, Thia came up with nothing. She was tired and bored, but if spycraft had taught her anything, it was that persistence paid off.

She decided to try battering nodes. Maybe Kappert's friends knew something and had a penchant to talk. Thia ran down the usual rectos and found the usual chatter—advice on node programming, news articles on quantum theory, announcement of a batter death. Arn Trumblis. Apparently dead after a sortie into American Hologram, which apparently used illegal military sentinels. The announcement called for a blitz on the company. Any and all interested batters were told to try and compromise their systems.

Interesting.

Thia tapped into the admin privileges and accessed the WP address of the recto post. It would take no time at all to match the addy and locate the address.

Bingo. District Heights, 700 block. Addy belonged to a Cor Wynst, not Chris Kappert. Still, it looked promising.

Midnight. Thia would get three hours' sleep, then leave to check on the address. Right now, she was tired. She spiraled out, then leaned back on the pillow and closed her eyes. As soon as she did, her incoming call light flashed, yellow cubes melding with red circles. Wu Ji. What did he want at this hour?

She winked open a line and the angular face of Wu Ji hovered over her. His usual brooding eyes held an unusual brightness, and a wry smile creased his face.

"This had better be good," Thia said.

"Hello to you, too."

"I'm on assignment, Ji."

"And I thought weekends were for me."

"Assignments take precedence."

"This will just take a couple hours. A company representative wants to buy enzo chips from a Chinese supplier. I need you to negotiate the deal."

"I don't even know what an enzo chip is."

"I'm hiring you for your negotiation skills, not scientific knowledge."

"What is it, anyway?"

"It eliminates enzymes from DNA samples."

"Whatever that means. Isn't it kind of late for a business deal?"

"It's under the radar."

"Where is it?"

"Downtown, Clinton Building. Columbia conference room, fifth floor."

"How much?"

"Five hundred thousand."

"Seven."

"All right. One a.m. I'll have my attorney meet you there with the papers. His name's Edor Fol. And be on time." Then he was gone.

Either Ji was in a hurry or this deal was really important. He hadn't even taken the time to try and bargain her price. Wasn't like him. Her curiosity was definitely piqued, but it looked as if it would be an all-nighter.

Thia rolled out of bed and grabbed a protein bar, wolfing it down on the way to her car. She kept a suit and a gown in the trunk for unexpected events. They also doubled as personal body armor, which had saved her on more than one occasion.

✿

The Clinton building boasted the city's only zero-energy system. Glazed mirrors reflected the surfaces of the surrounding buildings, which lent an oppressive air to the structure.

Thia wriggled in her navy suit as she pressed the button for the fifth floor, trying to shrug off the extra ten pounds of body armor. She only wore it when she would be walking into an unfamiliar, potentially dangerous situation. She didn't really want to be here, but the money was too good to pass up.

Not knowing the players, she was going in cold, but businessmen tended not to carry around heavy firepower—just their bodyguards, who were trained and predictable—so she felt relatively safe. But she'd rather be chasing down Nicholle, if nothing more than for the privilege of finding Wills and holding a pulser to his head. She could almost smell the fear in his sweat.

The elevator carried over the mirror theme, and she was treated to two full-length views of herself; the other two walls were decorated with faux green marble.

The doors opened and two beefy bodyguards stiffened. They flanked the entrance to the conference room, marked by a double faux green marble door. Thia calculated how she could take both of them with the bakepar shuriken hidden in her upswept hair, then smiled.

"I'm Tyra Thibodeaux," Thia said. "Here to negotiate the enzo chip deal."

"Mr. Zhao send you?" the guard on the left said.

"No, Mr. Ji."

"I'll need some ID."

"No problem." Thia opened her purse and rifled through her wallet, looking for the Thibodeaux ID card. It was nestled between Sanbora and Venat.

"Ah, here we go." She handed it to the guard, who inspected it with the intensity of a bondage club bouncer, then handed it back.

"We'll have to scan for weapons."

"But I see you have two weapons," Thia said, winking.

The guard looked away, but smirked as he pulled a metdet camera from his jacket and viewed her through the scope. She was wearing her chain mail underwear, and she enjoyed watching the guard's reaction to the view. It also didn't hurt that he didn't notice the trace metal in her shoe.

"Am I clear?" she said.

"All clear, ma'am. Welcome." He opened the door onto the proceedings and Thia stepped inside. The conference room was wood paneled, and the plush gold carpeting muted the voices of those inside. A rectangular wood table sat in the center of the room, flanked by eight chairs. A large translucent image of what Thia surmised was an enzo chip hung suspended in the air above the table.

How cheesy, she thought.

There were two men and one woman in the room, making it look as if she were the last to arrive. But they probably hadn't just gotten a phone call an hour ago telling them to show up. The woman was the first to approach. She had a confident stride, but she retained an air of malice about her.

"Hi, I'm Juna Hix. You must be Tyra Thibodeaux." She reached through the holographic chip to offer her hand and Thia wanted to squeeze it until the smirk on her face disappeared, but took her hand and shook it firmly.

"Why, yes I am. So nice to meet you." She affected a southern accent, which usually lulled people into thinking she was nice. "Can we turn this image off?"

"This is my partner, Ruyan Wexted, of Wexted, Hwan, and Chelo," Juna said. She motioned to the man sitting at the table, who got up and reached over for a handshake. He was tall with a potato-shaped face, receding hairline, and a quiet confidence that made him attractive. Thia exchanged pleasantries, letting her hand linger in his a second longer than necessary. He didn't seem in a hurry to let go.

She turned to meet the other man, who stood on the opposite side of the table. He had café au lait skin and shoulder-length dreadlocks, quite easy on the eye. If it weren't for the skank in the grey suit, she'd have been in hog heaven.

"I'm Edor Fol, attorney for Kunver Enterprises," he said.

"Pleased to meet you," Thia said.

"Well, shall we start?" Juna said.

Juna was rushing the meeting, a bad sign. Thia slipped off her jacket and threw it on one of the chairs. It was hot in the room, a common tactic to make the other negotiators lethargic, in this case her and Edor. Juna didn't know Thia had spent weeks in the Australian outback on survival training. She was going to have to do a lot better than this if she was going to fluster her.

"Just a moment to consult with Mr. Fol," Thia said.

Juna gave her a tight-lipped smile, but said nothing. Thia took Edor to the back corner to discuss the deal.

"Notice how hot the room is, and that they didn't even offer us anything to drink? They're trying to play psychological warfare. What's the maximum you want to pay for these enzo chips?" Thia said.

"They promised a deep discount, so we're willing to go to ninety million."

"How much are they usually?"

"About one hundred fifty million for a truck load."

"A forty percent discount. Do you usually traffic in stolen goods?"

Edor straightened, an indignant look on his face. "Certainly not."

"In denial, eh? Well, Wu Ji must like you because he sent me. Follow my lead and you'll be paying seventy-five."

"You seem rather confident."

"It's a rarefied air. Breathe deep and enjoy yourself." Thia strolled to the table and sat down, then spoke in a loud voice, interrupting Juna and Ruyan.

"Let's get started."

Juna gave her another tight-lipped grin, put her hand on Ruyan and whispered something to him, then came to the table and sat down. She crossed her hands in front of her.

"Getting comfortable already? Let's try to get this over with as soon as possible. I'm sure you're tired," Juna said.

Try staying up three days in downtown Copenhagen chasing some asshole terrorist, she thought. Tired was not being able to sleep because you had to hold a weapon on some lowlife scumbag all night to keep him from killing you.

"Not at all. In fact, I'm just getting warmed up. Now, you have some chips for sale. What's your price?" Thia said.

"Hm, straight to the chase. I like that. We're willing to sell at one hundred twenty million. And we can deliver on Friday or the following Monday. Which do you prefer?"

"That's cute, the old double option close. Listen, we're willing to pay fifty million for delivery on Friday. I think that's a reasonable offer."

"Fifty million? Surely you jest. We're talking Dyna8 chips, top-of-the-line merchandise."

"You mean stolen merchandise."

"Stolen? How dare you?" Juna paused to give Thia a nonverbal dressing down. "We offer a guarantee of satisfaction. How could we do that if the merchandise was stolen?"

"You didn't use the subjunctive. That tells me something, unless you're ignorant of its use. The timing of this meeting tells me another. Don't take me for a fool, Ms. Hix."

"No one's calling you a fool, Ms. Thibodeaux."

"I didn't say you were calling me one, I said don't take me for one. Sixty million, take it or leave it."

"I see you're not taking this deal seriously. Very well." Juna began gathering her papers. "We can deal with other companies. I'm sure there are—"

"Ms. Hix, please. Let me talk to Ms. Thibodeaux outside for a moment," Edor said.

Thia rolled her eyes, then clutched the table to push her chair away. She joined Edor outside the oak doors, down the hall from the two guards.

"What are you doing? We're about to lose the deal," Edor said. His face contorted, drawing his eyebrows together.

"Don't tell me you fell for that."

"I'm not about to take a chance on this. Either you close this deal, or I'm calling Mr. Ji."

Edor's back was facing the two guards, blocking their view of her. Thia reached in her pocket and extracted a switchblade, which she held to Edor's neck, pressing the blade into the soft underside of his jaw. The shocked look on his face told her he was unaccustomed to extreme negotiations.

"Listen, bitch. I'm the one calling the shots here. I'm the one Ji called." Thia spoke in a low voice. "I've got more important things to do than sit around all night, flapping my giblets, trying to save you a few million. Now,

K. Ceres Wright

you want this deal closed, fine. I'll close it. But don't piss me off, or they'll find your DNA on those little chips of theirs. Understand?"

Edor's silence and wide eyes gave her the answer she wanted. She lowered the blade, retracted it, and slipped it back into her pocket. Then she straightened her jacket and walked back down the hall, her heels clacking on the faux marble tile.

Thia flung open the oak door and paused, hand on her hip. "Ninety million, best and final offer."

"But—" Juna started.

"Do I have to repeat myself? I said best and final."

"I'll discuss it with my partner," Juna said. She got up and took Ruyan aside as Thia walked around to her side of the table. Edor stepped inside with a cautious look on his face. He sat down at the corner of the table, on the edge of the seat, far from Thia.

Thia drummed her fingernails on the table as she blew out a puff of air that lifted her bangs.

Juna finished consulting with Ruyan and sat down at the table opposite Thia. Her eyes flashed an air of arrogance that Thia wanted to squeeze out.

"We accept your offer."

"Good. Edor, pull out the—"

"But...at such a low price, we will have to revoke our guarantee."

"Revoke? You hadn't planned on offering it in the first place."

"I resent—"

"Just sign the papers so we can all go home." She'd had enough of this run-around.

Juna bit her lip, but retrieved a pen from her jacket and gathered the papers that Edor and Ruyan had placed on the table. All the parties signed, and the respective attorneys filed them away in their briefcases. Thia pushed away from the table and stood up.

"Nice doing business with you," she said.

"Quite. That was easier than the deal with Janice Brown," Ruyan said.

"Janice Brown? The personal attorney for Wills Ryder?" Thia said. The one he cheated on her with. Ho.

"Ye-es. You know her?" Ruyan said.

"Old friend of mine. We go way back, although I haven't spoken to her in a while. Did she buy chips for Wills, too?"

"I'm afraid I can't divulge any information. Attorney-client privilege, you know."

"Oh, I understand." She winked at Ruyan. "Well, I'd better be getting back to my hotel. Thank you, Juna, Ruyan, Edor. I hope this will be a profitable deal for all."

Edor held his peace as he shut the briefcase, barely giving her a glance. Thia stifled a grin, then left the room. The two guards were still eyeing her as the elevator doors shut.

Thia rode down to the parking garage and walked to her car. She climbed inside and sat, waiting for Ruyan to come down. What the hell would Wills want with enzo chips? She was determined to find out. Ruyan himself might not know, but he knew more than he was telling, and she meant to find out what.

After a couple games of sudoku to help keep herself awake, she saw Ruyan alight from the elevator with Juna. He seemed to be trying to persuade Juna to come with him, but she begged off. *Good.* He walked to a blue Javelin and got in.

She pulled behind him as he rounded the corner out of the garage. If he were an out-of-towner, it would be to her advantage, as he would probably be staying in the Taylor, which was just a few blocks away. If not, she might be in for a long drive to the purlieus.

Ruyan eased around the corner, down half a block, then pulled up to the valet parking in front of the Regal. Lazy ass, she thought. Still, the Regal was certainly no dive. It catered to those who could afford the steep price, usually rich diplomats and billionaire friends of the president. Why was a mere attorney here? Unless he was on the payroll of someone richer than his client.

She pulled up behind Ruyan and hopped out of the car, calling his name just as he was about to enter the hotel.

"Ruyan!"

He turned, his face registering surprise at first, then delight. Old guy was probably lonely. Thia slipped the valet a $1,000 bill. Normally they only let in guests who were staying at the hotel, but she kept area hotel and restaurant valets, hostesses, and waiters on her payroll. She had gotten more than one good tip from a waiter with an eagle eye.

"Miss Thibodeaux. I didn't know you were staying here," Ruyan said.

"I just checked in before I went to the meeting. Running late."

"That's easy to do in this area. Care to join me for a celebratory drink?"

"I'd be delighted." Thia wrapped her arm around Ruyan's and strode through the open doors. He led her over to the bar and pulled out her chair at a small table in a back corner. The shadow of the candle flame danced across the wall, licking the stucco as it went. A waiter appeared as soon as they were seated, and Thia wondered if word of her valet tip had made the rounds yet.

"What will you have?" Ruyan said.

"Scotch on the rocks."

"I'll have the same."

The waiter made a note in the air, then left. Thia caught the bartender's attention and put up two fingers. The bartender, Vas, nodded in reply. Ruyan leaned forward and began rubbing his five-o'clock shadow, a puzzled look on his face.

"He owes me one. I was just telling him I wanted these on the house," she lied. Vas would think she had just tracked down another pedophile and would mix in her special powder in his drink.

"A woman with connections. I like that. So where are you from?" he said.

"North Carolina, originally. But I live around here. I just stay here if I have business in town. A treat for myself." She interlaced her fingers and put her chin on her hands. Acting coy was not her strong suit, and she had to try hard to affect it.

"Well, we all need a treat now and then."

"Oh, you are so right, Ruyan." Thia slipped off her right shoe and slid her foot under the cuff of his pant leg. His socks were smooth, like Italian silk. As smooth as the bald spot on top of his head.

He chuckled in a low rumble. The waiter returned with their drinks and placed them on the small table, then left. Ruyan lifted his glass, prompting Thia to raise hers.

"To a long and profitable future," Ruyan said.

"Hear, hear."

Ruyan drank down half the glass, then licked his lips as he placed the glass on the table.

Fifteen seconds.

"Are you from around here?" Thia said.

"No, I'm from upstate New York. Town called Poughkeepsie. You heard of it?"

"Of course. I like to buy apples there in the fall, when I go up to look at the leaves. I think Yebedor lives there."

Ruyan's eyes glazed over and his movements slowed. Even though they were several tables away from the next group of customers, Thia spoke in a low voice.

"Tell me what business you have with Janice Brown."

"She bought enzo chips from our supplier for a project Mr. Ryder was working on." He spoke in a faraway, monotone voice.

"What project?"

"Something regarding a DNA computer."

"DNA?"

"Yes."

What was Wills up to? He was no biologist. He couldn't have invented a new form of life, or a cure for cancer.

Wills was smart. He knew how not to compromise himself, Thia thought. "What are you up to?"

"Trying to get you to go to my hotel room."

"Not you, you idiot." She took a sip of her drink. "Never mind." Thia leaned over and kissed Ruyan on the lips. He would be dead by morning.

She gathered her purse and left the bar, giving a generous tip to Vas on her way out. Nicholle was Thia's only lead now, and she meant to find her.

chapter 9

The small group rode in silence. Arn was dead. Nicholle squeezed her eyes closed to shut out the doctor's words, 'I'm sorry, but there's nothing more we can do.' Still. In this day and age, there was still nothing more to be done. Death always reaped its harvest.

Guilt was a vulture resting on her shoulder, eyeing her with a familial gaze. Welcome home, she thought. It's been a long time.

On the floor in Cor's basement, she had woken up with a headache that could have felled Paul Bunyan. They had all been out for several minutes, but when they checked on Arn, it was too late. He laid there with vacant eyes, mouth agape. They held onto hope as they were all taken to the hospital. Nicholle had given a fake name, denied permission to access her node. She checked out fine. Arn hadn't.

Trenar got out and slammed the door shut. Tears streamed down her face in rivulets of black. She ambled down the street toward the house. Nicholle wondered if someone should go to comfort her, but before she could say anything, another door slammed. Cor. He rapped once on the driver's-side window.

"Chris, can I talk to you?"

"Yeah, sure." Chris got out, leaving Nicholle in the passenger's seat. She didn't have to listen to know what Cor wanted to talk about. He wanted her out. And she could understand. They had taken her in, offered their help, and in return, received a trip to the hospital and a dead friend.

After a while, Chris returned and sat glum-faced in the driver's seat. Nicholle stared at Trenar until she disappeared from view around a corner. Cor ran after her.

"He wants us out," Nicholle said.

"Yeah."

"Can't blame him."

Chris put his hands on the steering wheel and lowered his head. Nicholle reached over and brushed the hair from his face. She had apologized at the hospital, more times than she remembered, and felt another apology would cheapen the meaning.

"You don't have to stay with me, Chris. Just drop me off at a homeless shelter. Go get a job at another company. Go on with your life. This is my battle, not yours."

He lifted his head. "It wasn't your fault, okay? And there's no way I'm leaving you. I signed up for this, remember? I could've said adiós after I saw the three dead bodies. But I didn't. Now, we just need a plan."

"Plan for what? Getting back my company? How are we going to do that in the situation we're in? My father's in a coma, I'm broke, my brother's in hiding, my other brother's trying to both kill and frame us, and I just got your friend killed, as well as my own."

"Your brother," Chris said.

"What about him?" Nicholle crossed her arms and leaned her head against the window.

"How do we know Perim didn't set him up, too?"

"Cuz with Wills, I could believe he actually did it."

"But that doesn't mean he'd set the company up to go bankrupt. You should cog him," Chris said. "Like he'd answer."

"Like he'd answer."

"We need answers. We need to know if he's to blame for this whole thing or not."

"If he was, do you think he'd tell me?"

"Maybe not, but at least make him look you in the face and tell you."

"Fine." Nicholle tapped open a line. "Call Wills Ryder."

A spiral blossomed into the image of Wills, pictured in a navy suit sitting at his desk at American Hologram. "I'm not in right now, but please leave a message, and I'll get back to you."

She almost closed the line, when Chris grabbed her hand.

"Wait. Maybe I can hack his node. Something with low security," he said. "We can use all the information we can get our hands on right now."

"What do I do?"

"Give me access to yours and I'll channel the call to mine."

She hesitated, but it wasn't as if she had much choice in the matter. They definitely needed any and all help. She reluctantly agreed.

"All right. But that's all you channel."

He rolled his eyes. "Don't worry. I'm not interested in the summer line from Paris."

"That's the spring-summer line, for your information."

She sat in silence while Chris went to work, trying not to drown in her own pity. If she ever got control of the company again, she'd make sure to hire Chris's friends and to give Arn's family an annual stipend for the rest of her life. Nothing could ever compensate, but if it helped, she'd be glad to give it.

A year ago, she would never think to do that. So into her own world, flipping with the high art crowd in New York—painters, sculptors, photographers, models. It was the life. But then it had all started to run together. The pakz, the parties, the schmoozing. The higher up she got, the more it was expected. And she had wanted to get high. And no better place than the fashion world. She had access to the rizzest designers, convinced the best artists to hold shows at her own gallery, and had even been the subject of several photographers' collections.

And then the Fall. And here she was—broke, tired, and guilty.

"I think I've got something," Chris said.

"What?" She perked up.

"Some memos. One's about a lunch date with two other executives, one's from some woman in Sudan. Man, he gets around. And here's one. Hello. From some guy with Nwanko Oil. He says he'll be at the meeting at the Port of Baltimore at six. He looks forward to being there. Tonight."

"Tonight? Sounds promising. Anyone else going?" she said.

"Yeah, some Leesia Fresno from Jiang Transport. Few others."

"Where's it going to be?"

"Fadi warehouse, Room A3."

"Sounds like a party."

"Then I guess we'll have to crash it," he said.

She closed the line. *What is he up to? Couldn't be business as usual.*

Her node chimed. Incoming. She answered the cog. The head of a man she had never seen before bobbled up. Grim-faced and disconsolate. An undertone of pain mingled with his voice.

"Are you Nicholle Ryder?"

"Who wants to know?"

"My name is Dr. Braxley Hagen of the Kryzo Hospice in Alexandria. I'm afraid I have—"

"My father," she said. She sat up, wanting to jump through his hologram.

"Yes, that's right. How did you know?"

"Because Dr. Lars at Washington District Hospital practically had him slabbed and out the door. I knew she would pull this. I'll have her license," she said.

"Ms. Ryder, Dr. Lars performed within the parameters of your father's wishes."

"Those were not his wishes. I know they weren't."

"Ms. Ryder—"

"How long does he have?"

"Seventy-two hours."

"Until Saturday," she whispered to herself. "I see. Well, I'll have proof that this whole thing was not his doing before then. That this is one huge mistake. And don't you touch him before then." She closed the line. Leaned forward, raking her fingers through her hair. Could it get any worse?

Swirls of orange and pink staccatoed her periphery. Incoming call: Wills Ryder.

She took a deep breath.

"It's Wills," she said. She opened the line.

"Wills."

"Nick." He was dressed in a light blue casual shirt, pictured against a beach backdrop.

"First you tell me where the hell you are and why you left." She couldn't believe he had the nerve to appear as if he were on holiday, enjoying fun in the sun after a hard day's work.

"I won't tell you where I am, but I will tell you that Perim set me up. I didn't call because I figured you were in on it, after I read that you had taken over the company."

"Chris asked me to take it over. I didn't want it."

"Seems he persuaded you rather quickly. I thought after your internship, you wouldn't darken the door to the company again."

"I'm doing it for Dad. Not me, not Chris, not you. And speaking of Dad, you haven't even asked how he's doing. He's in a coma with seventy-two hours left to live."

Wills paused. "Face it, Nick. We didn't really know Dad."

"What are you talking about? He's our father. He was there with us."

"When we were asleep. We saw him for five minutes in the morning. And when Mom was alive, we didn't even see him that much."

"He was there, Wills. Don't you remember?"

"The only thing I remember was the arguments he had with mom over his whoring around. Don't *you* remember?"

"Stop it, Wills. He's still our father." Her throat knotted, but she fought it down.

"Let's just get back to the subject at hand," she continued. "Perim framed me, too. He also took my money. I'm practically broke, and when we tried to hack into AmHo, he used military-grade sentinels and they killed someone."

"Shit. Wait…Nick, something's wrong. I'm picking up a sepsis being run on your node."

"A what?" Nicholle had picked up some terms from Chris on servers, programs, and computers, but this was a new one on her.

"It searches for information that meets certain criteria. Go offstream and get Chris to look at it. Stay safe."

He blanked and she spiraled out.

"My node." She turned to Chris. "A sepsis."

"A sepsis?" Chris looked as if she jerked him awake from a trance.

"Wills told me to spiral out. Perim sent it," Nicholle said.

"No. I've been monitoring their traffic, Perim and AmHo."

"Which means Wills just sent it." Her voice cracked when she said the words. She didn't want to believe it. Not her brother. Not after all they'd been through together as children. The thought of it weighed on her chest, a dull pain twisted.

"Can you delete it?"

"Already done."

"Why would he do that?"

"He's an ass, Nick. Can't you see? I mean I'm sorry, I know he's your brother, but him leaving like he did, dropping it in your lap, with your father in the hospital…that's just shitty. And you know it. You won't say it, but you know," Chris said. "What the…?"

"What?"

"Your brother's running off of another server. Nothing like I've seen. Not an RSFQ or CMOS. It's like…A, T, C, G. The DNA bases, right?"

"From what I remember, but what difference does it make?"

Chris looked straight ahead, no doubt decrypting the exchange she just had with Wills, teasing out any hidden code, tuning out reality.

That was his drug of choice, wiho. There had been some who fused their lives and personalities to it. Some who locked themselves in their room and didn't come out for months, being found near dead still spiraled in. Others had been found dead, some fresh, some close to mummification.

Every invention was someone's addiction.

She rolled down the window to let in some air. The fresh breeze blew in an autumn chill. And the barrel of a lazon appeared on the edge of the glass.

Nicholle gasped as the barrel swiveled to face her square on. She looked past the barrel to its holder. A woman—who seemed vaguely familiar. Auburn hair atop an angular face.

Nicholle put her hands up. "We don't have any money." She tapped Chris's shoulder to get his attention. Chris shrugged her off, but finally turned as her taps became more insistent.

"Shit!" he said. "We don't have any money."

"I don't want your money. Nicholle, in the back." She waved the gun. "Chris, I want you to take us somewhere."

"How do you know our names?" Nicholle said.

"I'm smart. Now move it!"

Nicholle clambered out of the front seat and fell onto the small bench seat in the back. The woman reached in and unlocked the door, then opened it and slid into the car, bringing with her the faint scent of alcohol.

"I suggest you hurry. To U Street, southeast."

Chris started the car and pulled away without another word, but his hands gripped the wheel with intensity.

"Who are you?" Nicholle said.

"Just call me Thia."

"Thia. So, ah, what is it you want?" Nicholle said.

"Information."

"Information? What kind of information?"

"The kind that lets me know where your brother is. When was the last time you heard from him?"

Nicholle's mouth gaped, then closed. "Last month."

The woman chuckled. "You're not a very good liar, Nicholle. But don't worry. I've got just the thing for you."

○

They pulled up in front of a row of abandoned, rundown buildings. Southeast. Nicholle wondered if the woman was going to take them out back and shoot them in the head. But if so, why? She knew their names, and obviously knew Wills. She had taken the time to do some research. Maybe Perim set her up, as well, and she had come looking for extreme justice.

97

Nicholle and Chris climbed a set of crumbling concrete steps to a squat building. The woman followed, holding the gun on both of them.

Shutters hung from windows, looking as if they might fall to the ground at any moment. The windows held screens that had large holes, offering an unobstructed view of broken glass panes. Nicholle shuddered to think what lay beyond that.

The grey door creaked as Chris opened it, and a strong odor of must blasted out. Nicholle began to cough, breathing in the dust whirling up. Her loud hacks echoed in the dim, empty hallway. She then sneezed loudly, twice, and wished her medinites would hurry and sweep away the offending material from her lungs and sinuses.

Chris must have thought Nicholle's coughing fit an appropriate time to go for Thia's gun, because he wheeled around and tried to knock it free with his arm. He pushed Thia's arm away, but Thia held fast to the gun and kicked Chris in the groin. He bent over and dropped to the floor, groaning.

"The hell do you think you're doing?" Thia said. She sneered at the prone figure.

"Chris!" Nicholle hurried over to him and cradled his head in her arms.

"How touching, but I think you're rubbing the wrong place. Now get up, the both of you, or he gets it in the kneecap." She squeezed off a shot that made a hole in the floor by Chris's knee and seared his pants leg.

Nicholle jumped. "Stop it!"

"Then get up."

Nicholle got to her feet, then helped Chris up. He was bent at the knee and back, but he managed to scuffle down the hall. At the end of the hall was an elevator door. Thia pressed her thumb in a small indentation in the frame and the door opened.

Nicholle had expected a rundown elevator car with peeling paint and a take-your-life-in-your-hands ride. Instead, the door opened onto gleaming stainless steel and a robotic assistant—about four feet tall with a square head and torso and treads for legs.

"Agent XH11, how may I assist you?"

"Take us down to the play room, J9," Thia said.

The assistant fell silent, then the elevator plummeted before coming to a slow stop. The door opened onto a laboratory. J9 led the group past large tables outfitted with robotic arms that shuffled various beakers and tubes back and forth, pouring the contents into other containers.

They walked past the arms and came to a door at the far end of the lab. J9's transparent head lit up and the door opened. The cleanliness of the laboratory did not carry over. The back room had a concrete floor, dirty yellow walls, and a single old-fashioned bulb that hung from a wire in the middle of the room.

Thia pushed Nicholle inside and she stumbled over a pile of sackcloth bags. The smell from the bags overwhelmed her, even from a distance. A table stood in the middle of the room, covered with various tools. Pressure settled in the middle of her chest and her scalp began to tingle.

"What is that smell?" She spoke to help quell her fear.

"You'll find out. You, in there." Thia waved the gun at Chris, motioning him toward another room. He edged inside and the door quickly shut behind him.

"Make sure he doesn't get out," Thia told the robot.

J9 stood by the door and fell silent. Its lights darkened except for a single blinking yellow dot in the middle of its head.

"Tell me where Wills is," Thia said.

"I don't know."

"Put one of those bags on your head."

Nicholle looked with disdain at the pile of bags and the smell emanating from them. "But I really don't know."

"Now!" Thia squeezed off a shot, which seared past Nicholle, singeing the side of the table. She picked up a bag and put it on her head. The smell was horrifying, filling her nose and mouth. She gagged.

"What the hell is this?"

"Yak piss."

"Yak piss? You are a sick..." Nicholle coughed deeply. "...bitch."

"Put these on." Thia threw something at Nicholle that clacked like metal on the hard concrete at her feet. Nicholle bent over to retrieve it.

"Handcuffs?" she said.

"Now!" Thia said.

Nicholle fumbled with them as the stench filled her nostrils and crowded her senses. A series of clicks, then they fastened around her wrist.

"Now what? Ah-AHH!" The air ripped, and a burning pain shot across Nicholle's back, cleaving her skin. She fell to her knees, open-mouthed and silent. Warm blood trickled, soaking her shirt. Short gasps escaped her lungs, but hardly a sound, as the pain wended its jagged way home.

"Nicholle! Leave her alone! Don't you touch her! Nicholle!" Chris pounded on the door of his small room. His muffled commands comforted her, even if they went unheeded.

"Where are the plans for transfer of consciousness?"

"What are you talking about?" Nicholle said. "AAAHH!" Another lash cut across her back, ripping up cloth, skin and flesh. More blood soaked her shirt and it stuck to her back in a wet, clammy mass. She swam in pain, gulping in deep breaths of it, along with the yak urine as she fell forward, onto her elbows.

"I...don't know anything. My brother...never tells me about the business."

"Why don't I believe that? Come on. Something that'll make the rich richer? I know you're interested in that," Thia said. "Even an art dealer like yourself. Rich bitch."

"You're the...bitch. Who the hell are you, anyway? Some crazy whore my brother screwed and dumped? Take a number. There's plenty more where HAAAA!"

The pain lashed harder this time. Nicholle figured she hit a nerve with Thia. Flaming shards of white lanced across her vision. The agony forced her flat on the floor and the muscles in her arms began to spasm. She was losing medinites in the blood flow, but they were giving her some relief.

"Where are the plans for consciousness transfer?"

She kept asking for that. If Wills had discovered it, then it was no wonder Perim wanted them all out of the way. *Bastard.* So that was it. And this crazy bitch probably wanted it for herself.

"All right! I'll tell you." Essence of yak filled her mouth and she spit against the sackcloth. The saliva dribbled down the sackcloth and onto the front of her shirt.

"It's on the AmHo node. But the vice president locked me out, so you're going to have to hack into it. Look for the corporate security subnode, then Wills Ryder's personal node. It's there, marked File Thirteen."

"Password?"

Any one would do. She wouldn't get that far anyway, thought Nicholle. "Constantine."

"Well, I see the cat has conquered another victim. She never fails." Thia laughed. Nicholle didn't know if she was talking about the whip or herself.

Nicholle heard the door open and close and figured Thia had gone out to get a fryer. She took the urine-soaked bag off her head and spat several times, then took in deep breaths of fresh air. The J9 unit stood still next to the door, unfazed by Chris's incessant pounding.

Thia walked into the room with a fryer on her head. She waggled her finger at Nicholle.

"Tsk tsk. I didn't say you could take off the bag. But since you've been such a good girl, I'll let you slide. Now, watch the downfall of American Hologram." Thia activated the controls on the fryer and began her sortie.

Nicholle watched in anticipated horror. Seeing people die, or at least writhe in pain, wasn't easy. Not even, she guessed, when it was a tormentor.

Thia performed a series of finger movements, then froze, a half-smile on her face. She dropped to her knees, bucked, and fell to the ground, face first. Her forehead hit the concrete with a dull thud; her right leg began to twitch, then stopped. The military sentinels had done their work, earned their pay for the week.

"Thanks, Perim. You were good for something." Nicholle stood up, keeping a wary watch on J9. She didn't know if it had AI. Regular robots were dumb.

They only did what you told them. Nicholle slid toward Thia and reached to get her lason, keeping watch on the robot. It remained still. The powerpak on the lason indicated it was half-loaded. But it might have been programmed for Thia's use only, and Nicholle didn't want to take a chance with a robot. She'd have to use Thia's hand.

On the table was a long curved piece of metal with a serrated edge. She walked slowly over to the table, keeping an eye on the robot. The metal gleamed in the dull light, as if it had been polished after each use. She could picture Thia lovingly shining it after sawing off someone's genitals.

Nicholle made her way to the table, facing the robot, and reached behind her as she lifted the blade, then stepped over to Thia and kneeled down. She took the woman's right hand and began to cut.

Blood seeped onto the floor, pooling at her knees and soaking her pants. The blade caught when she reached bone and Nicholle anchored the arm by kneeling on Thia's palm. She leaned over the blade, bearing down as she sawed on.

"Nicholle? Is that you? What's going on?" Chris asked.

"Hold on."

When she got her prize, she held it by the fingers and tapped off as much blood as she could. It splattered on the floor and across Thia's body. She picked up the gun and placed it in Thia's hand. She positioned the fingers, but there wasn't enough room on the trigger for both index fingers, so Nicholle had to insert her pinky, which made it awkward. Still, she would have the element of surprise. Or so she hoped.

She crawled behind the table and aimed the gun at J9. Thia's cut-off wrist proved a gruesome sight, but she looked past that to J9's head. It would be gone in a minute. She squeezed the trigger, but nothing happened. Except J9 must have detected a weapon directed at it. Its head lit up and turned toward Nicholle.

"Crap." She overturned the table in time to block a plasma blast. Nicholle grabbed a hammer and chucked it at the robot. It shot the tool out of the air. She ducked back behind the table.

"Glad it wasn't my head."

J9 began to move toward her. On the floor next to her were two metal clamps attached to rubber wires that led to an electrical device. No doubt another tool for genital torture. She grabbed the clamps and threw them over by Thia's body, then dragged the worktable so J9 would have to go around it to get at her. Which meant it would roll into—

Nicholle switched on the electricity, sending a current through the pool of Thia's blood.

J9 sparked and the blood sizzled, splattering on the worktable. The robot lit up and flickered on and off, then crashed into the wall. Its lights dimmed and died.

Nicholle snatched up Thia's severed hand and shook it off the gun. She ran to the door and inserted Thia's thumb in the slot and the door opened.

"Nicholle. Are you all—" He noticed the severed hand and took a step back.

"I had to cut it off to shoot the robot with the gun, but the gun didn't work, so I had to electrocute it."

Chris gaped, then swept Nicholle up in his arms. "Thank goodness you're all right."

Nicholle sank into his muscled embrace, savoring the smell of his cologne. The threat of finality had an aphrodisiac effect on her, and she nestled her head in the crook of his neck. He pushed her away, his face drawn up in disdain.

"Oh, yeah, yak urine."

"Let's get out of here," he said.

○

They drove up Route 301, searching for someplace to settle for the night. The strains of Bach filled the space between them, along with the faint scent of lavender mingled with urine. They rode in silence as Nicholle processed the day's events. Chris offered a few comments, but only garnered a grunt in reply.

Chris passed by the famous hotel chains, knowing they would require cogin for a deposit. They needed a place that would ask few questions and accept cash. The Blue House Motel beckoned with its shabby exterior and neon sign that announced vacancies. It rested on the edge of a copse of trees on a patch of land between the northbound and southbound lanes. The exterior coat of blue paint gave off an iridescent sheen under the nearby floodlights.

"This looks promising," Chris said. He slowed and eased into the lot. "Wait here."

"Hmm," Nicholle said. She didn't have to be persuaded to stay in the car. As Chris went inside, a woman wearing nothing but a towel spilled out of one of the rooms. She held a cigarette in one hand and the towel in the other.

"I tole ya ya left it inna car!" she said. She stumbled to a dirty white car, opened the door, and began rummaging in the front seat.

"Git ma beer, too!" echoed from inside the room.

The woman closed the car door, hauling a bag, with the cigarette clasped firmly at the edge of her mouth. She ambled back to the room and kicked the door closed.

"Old-fashioned doors," Nicholle mumbled. She jumped when Chris opened the door to the car.

"C'mon. We're in room 3."

chapter 10

Lights twinkled across the horizon, covering the Baltimore landscape. Towering orange cranes huddled over the Port of Baltimore, transferring cargo from the ships hugged against the docks to the colorful containers that dotted the sea port. The scene loomed larger as the car approached the port, a brilliant vista viewed from the I-95 bridge.

Chris had uploaded altered photos and IDs for them, son and niece of the foreign diplomat who was the registered owner of the car. She checked the status of her father, but he remained unchanged. She almost called the doctor, but she could never be ready to hear from a doctor who said that her father only had two days to live. *Hard to fathom.* And if she dwelled on it, she'd be unable to function. So she put it out of her mind, at least as much as she could. She thought hard of something else.

Nicholle wondered why Wills had called the meeting with reps from bio research, pharmaceuticals, and aeronautics. They had nothing to do with wiho.

Diversifying, Wills? And why a warehouse?

Warehouses were cold, dirty affairs, not plushly outfitted conference rooms with wet bars and catered gourmet food. He was that spoiled. Before a meeting, his aide would send a list of particulars to meeting coordinators, demanding imported water, Dutch licorice, and Moribel cognac. She doubted they had Dutch licorice and aged cognac within the metal hull of a warehouse.

"This brings back memories. I grew up in Baltimore," Chris said.

"Near the docks? Did the sailors tell you stories from distant lands?"

Chris laughed. "No. I lived in the county. But some weekends my dad would take me to go get a chili dog and we'd come down here to watch the ships. He used to work the docks and said it was a treat to watch other people working."

"If I worked here, I think it'd be the last place I'd want to come on the weekends." Nicholle shifted in her seat, relieving the leg that had fallen asleep. She remembered the docks, as well. Waiting for shipments of pakz, which she helped divide up to deliver to those who couldn't afford skeemz.

"No. He loved this place. It was his life. He worked here for thirty years. Knew everybody." Chris slowed the car as they came to a red light. "He even died here," he added in a quiet voice.

Nicholle angled a look. "Oh, I'm so sorry. You okay to come here?"

"Oh, yeah. Just a little, you know. Like I said, brings back memories."

"Can I ask you something?"

"Anything."

"What was it like? Losing your father."

Chris drew in a breath and exhaled slowly. "It was, at first, so surreal. I didn't believe it. Then after the funeral, it began to sink in, and I'd never felt so alone. We were close."

We weren't close. Wills had always reminded her of that, over her denials. But in that, Wills was right. She finally had to admit it. She had wanted to believe they were a typical family with its share of typical problems, but she was finally beginning to see the dysfunction.

The car behind them honked and Chris accelerated past the green light. They pulled up to a sentinel gate lined with secbots, which could fry the car if their limited AI found anything overtly suspicious.

"If you are not an employee, please turn your vehicle around and exit the premises," the holographic guard said.

Nicholle placed her hand on Chris's arm as the memory self-resurrected from stasis.

"I know where we can go. Drive toward Dundalk. I'll give you directions along the way," she said.

Chris glanced sideways, the space between his brows folded in annoyance.

"And tell me we won't get kidnapped and nearly killed this time," he said.

His reaction bruised what sense of confidence she still had left. The confidence she needed to help get them inside.

"What? You act like that whole ordeal was my fault. I had no idea she was after us."

Chris turned the car around and followed the sign to the main road, veering left. "She was after us to get to Wills for some experiment she believes he's conducting. Only I've never known Wills to conduct experiments, and she seemed to be well connected with access to high-tech areas, so I don't think she was crazy. Well, *completely* crazy. She found us easily enough, and I think it's entirely possible she knew something that we didn't, namely, what the hell it is that Wills is up to."

Since Nicholle had time to process recent events, Chris's musings were beginning to make sense. Nothing normal had occurred since Monday night, at least not from her perspective. *So maybe it's time to think from a different perspective.*

"Make the next right," she said. "So what if Wills somehow discovered the secret of transferred consciousness…downloaded personalities, whatever you want to call it. What would the implications be?"

They pulled into a neighborhood of brick row houses. Generations of entrenched families had stabilized the area, staving off the typical suburban decay. Streetlights lit the way. In other suburbs, they would have long since been broken.

"Second right, third house on the left," she said.

Chris obeyed and pulled in front of the specified house. He shut off the engine and leaned back against the head rest.

"Jeez, Nicholle, they'd be staggering. Never really having to die…if you get a disease, you can just upload to a new body. Although whose body would you upload to? I doubt you could upload to a dead body and have it work. And most people are already using their own bodies."

Nicholle bolted upright in her seat as realization dawned. "Oh, my god. People in comas," she whispered. She faced Chris, hand over her mouth, tears welling in her eyes. The thought offended her. She tried to put it out of her mind, but it edged back, around the corners of her defenses. "My father."

Chris grabbed her by the shoulder and squeezed. "I think you're letting your imagination run away with you. Think about it. How could Wills put your father in a coma?"

She shook her head. "I don't know."

"So let's not jump to conclusions. We're here. What now?"

Nicholle smeared the tears across her face until they dried, until her medinites mopped up the ones beneath the surface.

"There are tunnels that lead from three of these houses over to warehouses at the terminal. They're usually guarded, but we may be able to create a diversion. Loud music coming from the car, I'm thinking. They don't want to bring attention to the area, so they'll probably come outside to shut it down. We can hide in the bushes and jump inside as he's walking to the car. Tuma's kinda cheap, so there should only be one guard."

Chris heaved a sigh and rubbed his forehead. "You think this will work?"

"We don't have much choice. Feel free to offer another idea, though."

Her suggestion was met with silence.

"Plan A it is, then," she said. "Pop the trunk. I'll get the bag. You sync with the car for remote control."

Nicholle climbed out of the car, grabbed the bag, and slung it over her shoulders.

As Tuma's men were not landscapers, the bushes in front of the house were unkempt and large enough to hide both of them. They crouched, Nicholle toward the corner of the front steps, and waited. The bushes pressed against her, scratching through her sweater. Chris tapped up the command, rolled down the windows to the car, and turned the speakers all the way up on a horror movie. Stomach-churning screams pierced the quiet, along with loud banging, like someone breaking in a door.

In the dark, Nicholle gave Chris a thumbs up. Muffled voices wafted from inside, then heavy footsteps. They bounded on the floor, stopped at the door. Door squeaks, then a bang as the screen door closed. Boots pounded the concrete steps. Neighbors' voices yelled out windows.

"Now," Nicholle said. She and Chris grabbed the railing above and pulled themselves up, then scrambled over. A quick glance told Nicholle the guard was about to lason the dashboard. They ducked inside and Nicholle led Chris to the back of the house. She turned into a small bathroom and motioned Chris inside.

Nicholle pressed one end of the towel rack and the toilet slid to one side, revealing a dark hole underneath. She crouched, then swung her legs inside and caught the ladder beneath.

"There's a ladder here on the back wall," she said before climbing down. Chris followed her. When he reached the bottom, she twisted a knob on the wall at the bottom of the ladder and the light overhead disappeared as the toilet swung back. Complete darkness surrounded them, pressing in like curtains through an open window.

"Is there a light?" Chris said in a low voice.

"There is, but turning it on alerts the guard upstairs," Nicholle said. "But don't worry, I remember this tunnel. It goes on straight for about fifty yards, dips down, then curves to the right for another twenty, straightens, then inclines upward. Follow me and keep your right hand on the wall to help give you a sense of direction."

"Okay."

Nicholle led the way, stepping quickly along, unsure of whether the guard upstairs would suspect something and come to inspect. There were side tunnels they could duck into, but they were farther up the passageway. The air was surprisingly fresh and she guessed Tuma had installed a ventilation system. She had suggested it to him in case, for whatever reason, someone was stuck down there for a period of time. She'd also suggested some doomsday supplies for food, but she didn't know if he'd taken her up on that one.

The tunnel dipped, then curved, and they followed it. The faint scraping of ceramic against wood echoed in the tunnel and Nicholle's heart quickened. She reached back along the wall for Chris's hand and took it in hers as she hurried to get to the first side tunnel, trotting on tiptoe. Chris mimicked her moves as the sound of his hurrying lightened. Boots on wood sounded behind them, descending the ladder.

Just up here. Please, please.

The lights came on in the tunnel, illuminating the smooth dirt walls that led up to the silver ventilation piping that ran along the ceiling. The side passage lay about a yard ahead.

"Hey!" the guard said. He could not see them, because Nicholle could not see him in the curve of the space. He probably wasn't sure anyone was in the tunnel, she thought, else he would not have called out. If he knew they were there, however, he would start running after them, shooting.

Nicholle turned into the side tunnel and pulled Chris along. She stopped and leaned against the wall, waiting. Chris stared at her, but she put her finger to her lips, gesturing for him to remain silent. The lights stayed on, which meant the guard was still in the tunnel. Nicholle's heart pumped faster and she tried to quell her anxiety.

She had learned a few self-defense moves from one of Tuma's guards, Brock, a year ago when they were both working the docks one uneventful night. Nicholle struggled to recall what he taught her as she edged around Chris. She crouched low and motioned for Chris to do the same. His face contorted in a disbelieving look and he caught her by the shoulder to pull her back, but she shrugged him off and gestured for silence.

The guard's steps padded softly on the impacted dirt. Her breathing came in shallow sips as she strained not to make noise. His steps edged closer and she waited for the exact moment. The padding became louder.

Now.

The guard stopped and turned, holding a lason. Nicholle lunged. He fell backward, hitting his head on the wall opposite. The weapon discharged, shooting past her shoulder. She hoped Chris hadn't been in the line of fire. Nicholle grabbed the man's arm and struggled to keep the weapon pointed upward. A loud snap sounded.

"Ahhhhhh!"

The man hollered and his arm fell limp. Nicholle wrestled the gun out of his hand and rolled off of him. Chris stood on the man's foot with his full weight, bouncing on the broken bone. As soon as Nicholle rolled off, he snatched the man by the shirt and delivered five blows to his head.

The guard fell, unconscious, to the floor. Chris shook his right hand, fingers splayed, seemingly in pain. Nicholle wanted to remain on the floor and sleep away the nightmare that was her life, but she had too much responsibility to give up.

"C'mon," Chris said. He held out a hand. She reluctantly took hold and braced herself to standing.

"At least we've got a weapon," he said.

Nicholle nodded as she snapped on the safety and tucked it in the back of her pants.

"Let's get going," she said.

They walked swiftly down the tunnel. The other end of it had a ladder similar to the first one. Nicholle twisted the knob on the wall and switched off the lights.

"There's no guard on this end. It opens into a supply closet, behind a shelving unit," she said. Chris nodded and climbed up. Nicholle followed, then shut the opening behind her.

"The Fadi warehouse is..." She strained to remember. "Two warehouses over. Take your shirt out of your pants and put on one of these tool belts."

She hauled the belts off the shelf and handed one to Chris.

"I'm not exactly dressed for industrial cleaning," he said.

"Doesn't matter. It's dark and we're only going over two warehouses. Should be pretty much deserted. This time of night, most of the activity is over by the port cranes."

They fastened their belts and threw on brimmed caps that had the port logo on the front. Chris took hold of a supply cart and pushed it through the door Nicholle held open.

"We should talk loudly and laugh, not look around suspiciously," Nicholle said.

"Good idea." He raised his voice. "So I was in this bar, right, and this chick comes up to me and says, 'Wanna get outta here? Go someplace quiet where we can talk?' Well, I'm a little drunk, so I'm not thinking straight, so I say, 'Sure.' So we leave out the back, only when I walk out the door, two guys club me over the head. The next thing I remember, a dog licking my face, my wallet's gone, my wedding ring is gone, and even my belt is gone. So I gotta call my wife to come get me and explain how I got jumped, only all she can ask is what I'm doing in the alley in the first place."

"Oh, yeah?" Nicholle said. "So what'd you tell her?" They had gone out the door and were halfway across the first warehouse. Two people smoking cigarettes looked their way, but went back to their conversation.

"I said I had just stopped by the club for a few drinks after work, to unwind, you know?"

"Yeah, yeah. Unwind. Everybody needs to unwind."

"That's what I told her," Chris said. "Only she says she's tired of my wandering ways and wants a trial separation."

"What? Over a drink?" Nicholle said. They edged toward the second warehouse and Nicholle opened the door as Chris pushed the cart through. The warehouse was vast, the length of a football field. Paned windows lined the perimeter of the building. Black frame rafters checkerboarded the ceiling. Containers stacked in precise rows of ten high, ten wide stood in the middle of the floor. No one was around, at least not yet.

"So'd you go through with it?" she said.

"One week into it. It's rough, you know?"

Nicholle put her hand on the cart and led him to an alcove that held an elevator. She pushed the down button.

"Offices are in the basement," she said in a low voice. "What room was the meeting in?"

"A3," he said.

The elevator doors opened and Nicholle and Chris went inside. Black metal shined to a mirror finish edged in silver enveloped them. Neither spoke on the ride down. When the door opened, Nicholle motioned to her right. Chris followed.

Beige carpeting lined the hallway, and original art hung on the wall. Nicholle gasped.

"Look. A Yebedor oil. I've never seen this one before."

"We don't have time to sightsee."

"Yeah, yeah," she said. Annoyance crept into her voice. It had been a harrowing past few days and the tension was catching up to her.

She headed down the hall and checked the offices. Behind the first three doors were Spartan rooms, containing little more than a desk and chair. She opened the door to the fourth office and was struck by the sight of bright marigold walls. A heavy cherry wood desk sat in front of the far end. A backlit glass insert lined the wall next to the desk, displaying imported water and Moribel cognac. A sofa and loveseat framed a small coffee table and a crystal dish of what looked like licorice rested on the desktop.

"Bingo," Nicholle said.

She left the room and waved Chris into the office next to Wills'.

"Let's hide in the closet the next door over," she said.

They sat in the closet in Room A2 and squeezed the cart in front of them. If someone opened the closet, they would not be immediately visible.

"What now? How do we spy on Wills from the next office over?" Chris said.

"This place should have hidden cameras. Can you access them?"

"If it's wi, it's mine."

"That so?"

"You know it."

Nicholle sat in thought as Chris scanned. The memo didn't specify the purpose of the meeting. She wondered what game Wills was playing.

"Got it," Chris said. "There *are* hidden cameras in each of these rooms. I can link to the cameras in Wills' office and feed the image to my node. So spiral in." He worked quickly, looking like the Morse code operator on board the *Titanic*. "Okay. I've established the link. The feed should be coming in as soon as someone enters the office. The camera's activated by motion."

"By motion? Then what about the one in here?" Nicholle said.

"I've disabled the one in here and deleted the feed since just before we arrived."

"So now we wait."

"Now we wait," Chris said. He paused, regarding her with a curious stare.

"What?" she said.

"You know, there were rumors a year or so ago. I chose to ignore them..."

"But you wondered if they were true," she said. Nicholle expected for the news to get out and, in fact, was surprised it hadn't been blared across the news landscape. She guessed her father had something to do with it.

"I started doing pakz and skeemz about two years ago, and I hit the street about a year back. My addiction had gotten out of hand. I made mistakes. My gallery went downhill. Hell, everything went downhill. To keep up my addiction, I had to...well, compromise myself. Had to run pakz, rack skeemz, sex up pakz suppliers, just to get froze on skeemz. Skeemz cost, but they're safer, being programs and all. But even froze, I rose in the ranks, so to speak. Became an associate, a gofe, working for the Tets."

"The Tets? Isn't that one of those secret societies or some choo like that?"

"Yeah, well, they ain't that secret. Mostly greedy businessmen looking for a quick profit, spouting some semblance of a higher purpose. They use local talent to run the day-to-day. But they're safer than the street gangs, and a lot richer. Although some of the gang and Tet gofes move in the same circles."

"And they run pakz?"

"Pakz, women, weapons, skeemz on the lower level. Lobbying, bribes, and corporate theft on the upper. The Shantou/Bank of Nigeria conglomerate's got them running scared, so from last I heard, they were looking to expand."

"How'd you get out?"

"I made the mistake of calling my brother for money. He gave me an ultimatum. I took it."

They fell into silence. Nicholle wondered what Chris thought of her now…if he would have agreed to go with her if he had known. She couldn't worry about it now, she thought. That was water under the bridge; she couldn't change the past.

They did not have to wait long before someone showed up. A brown-skinned man appeared in life-like miniature holoform between her and Chris. *Wills.* He shrugged off his trenchcoat, hung it on the back of the door, and took out a fryer from the desk drawer. He began tapping up commands.

"Looks like he's accessing the admin functions of something. Maybe the DNA server? Setting controls. And he's out," Chris said.

Wills took off the fryer and placed it back in the drawer. After a few moments, there was a chime at the magfield door.

"Come in," Wills said.

The field went transparent and a woman stepped through. Her hairline began halfway down her forehead. A harsh line of blush ran from her cheeks to her ears.

"Leesia. Good to see you." He kissed her cheek.

"William. And you. I must admit, I was surprised to hear from you. The news says you embezzled from the company trough and left town. You naughty boy." She held up a finger and waggled it at him.

"Don't tell me you believe what you hear in the news. I had a scheduled meeting in Fiji and am just getting back. But more on that when the others get here. Please, sit down. Drink?"

"Yes, white wine, thanks," Leesia said.

"Coming up." The wall parted behind his desk, revealing a large bar. As he prepared the drink, the magfield chimed again.

"Must be the others. Come in," he said. He handed Leesia her drink. The magfield faded. Two men strode inside. One had cheekbones sculpted from marble, inset over dark hollows. Hawkish eyes drew a bead on all surveyed. The other man possessed an understated confidence, evident in his swagger.

"Nwanko, Tawd. Glad you could make it. Have a seat and let's see. Scotch on the rocks and a Guinness?" Wills asked.

"William playing the host? This must be important. I have a feeling we're about to get our asses handed to us," Nwanko said.

Tawd chuckled. "So what's the bad news?" He sat on the loveseat next to Leesia, grinning.

"Lovely as always, Leesia," he said.

"Flatterer."

"Just one more guest and we can get down to business," Wills said. He delivered the drinks and sat on the edge of his desk, observing the others making small talk.

Nicholle knew that look. It meant he was sizing someone up, just before a fight, whether mental, verbal, or physical. Something was about to go down, and she was sure the others wouldn't like it, but there wasn't a thing they could do about it.

Wills hopped down from his desk at the sound of the chime with a self-satisfied smile. When the magfield faded, another woman stepped inside. Tall, with a gap-toothed smile and a trusting face.

"Darai! Welcome," Wills said. They kissed in greeting.

She took up a seat on the couch next to Nwanko.

"Sherry, right?" Wills asked.

"Yes, you remembered."

"Of course." The other guests greeted her as if they had been bosom buddies.

"All right, now we can cut to the chase. Why are we all here?" Nwanko said.

"Patience, my friend." Wills resumed his seat on the edge of the desk.

"First of all, I'd like to thank you for coming tonight. I know all of you are busy, but I think this business opportunity is one you can't afford to pass up."

"Don't tell me you're selling insurance," Leesia said. Good-natured laughter followed. Wills maintained a tight-lipped smile.

"Actually, in a way, I am. Do you know what happened when cars were first invented? Automobile manufacturers were competing directly with horse-and-buggies. That is, until the gas engine car was improved upon, forcing the carriage makers out of business. Many of them tried to get financing to get into the car trade, but they couldn't. And so, we see how technology can change the landscape of the business world.

"Today, we're at the dawn of a new age. And I'm here to say, that the more things change, the more they remain the same."

Nicholle rolled her eyes. Wills was a blowhard, through and through, which was rare for a scientist, but perfect for a businessman.

"Cut the bull and tell us about this so-called opportunity," Tawd said.

"Very well. I assembled a team of scientists to accomplish a task for me and they have almost succeeded."

"Succeeded at what?" Darai said.

"Transfer of consciousness. In other words, download your personality into another body."

Leesia choked on her drink while the others stopped in mid-motion, staring wide-eyed at Wills, who was grinning like a pundit who successfully predicted the scandal-of-the-week.

"Are you serious?" Darai said.

"How has it been tested?" Tawd said.

"Let's just say, compromises had to be made," Wills said.

"That smells like a class-action lawsuit," Nwanko said. Nervous laughter.

"The reason I brought you here is that each of you is the head of a company whose industry will likely be affected by this. At least directly—medical, pharmaceutical, and aeronautics. Companies that will be transformed once I introduce this invention to the marketplace. Which means we all need to work together to perfect the process and establish a multiphased educational, social, and promotional campaign," Wills said.

"You expect people to flock to an unproven method of transfer, where they'll be in danger of getting their consciousness scrambled?" Leesia said. "It'll never be accepted."

"Oh, this is just the start of a long-term project, my dear. We have yet to achieve a fully successful transfer, but I'm working on downloading to adult clones who don't have the baggage of a past life."

Nwanko stood up and walked to the bar to pour another drink. "Cloning is illegal. And the Senate would never approve it."

"This is madness. No such thing exists. I'd have to see it to believe it," Tawd said.

"In time, Tawd, in time. I'm working with a senator to introduce legislation on cloning. It will be a process, as I said. First we'll introduce a bill addressing therapeutic cloning, even as we continue conducting the experiments. Once that bill passes, it will open the gates for additional legislation. Imagine…people with debilitating diseases can start life again with a healthy body. Can you imagine the PR for that? The elderly can have the wisdom of an 80-year-old in a 20-year-old body. And does it take more than a lifetime to travel to the closest star? No problem. Stay in storage and download upon arrival. So…what do you say?"

The guests looked warily at each other, some fidgeting. Darai was the first to speak.

"Well, Wills, this is certainly intriguing, but I'd have to see clinical trials evidence, information that guaranteed the safety of the, uh, recipient, so to speak. I'm sure we could talk next week—"

"There will be no next week. This is a one-time offer, that expires in ten minutes," Wills said. "The price for investment is ten trillion. So make your decision."

"It would be impossible for me to make such a decision tonight. I'm afraid I'll have to decline." Darai stood up, placed her drink on the table, and headed for the door. Wills pulled a lason from his jacket and fired. She arched back as her legs splayed. Her knees bent and she crashed to the floor.

Leesia screamed as they all stood up, their faces blank masks of shock.

"Does anyone else want to back out?" Wills said. He looked each one in the eye. "Make your decision now."

Nwanko shook with anger. "This is madness."

"Isn't that what they say to all geniuses? Explain it any way you like, but just make sure you transfer the money. If you have to sell stock, I have a handy broker access code that we can all use, so step right up."

"How do you expect to explain Darai's death? Even if we sell our stock, we could still go to the police," Tawd said.

"Not if you're in danger of being implicated in it. You were on the scene. Why? I'm sure your stockholders would love to find out. In addition, let's just say I have an army, and I know where each of your children attend school. But why make it difficult? Just transfer the money, and you'll be free to go."

"Do we have your word?" Tawd asked.

"Of course." Wills said, smiling.

The remaining three executives tapped up commands, sold stock, and transferred the money to Wills' account. Then Wills shot them. Four bodies lay strewn in the office, all burnt through with a charred hole in the middle. Nicholle had seen people get shot before, but this was different. This wasn't a pakz sale gone bad, where people knew what the deal was before it went down. These poor people had been presented with an impossible offer, then...executed.

After he was done, Wills put on his trenchcoat and walked out of the office, leaving the bodies there. Presumably to be cleaned up by someone else.

A dull ache filled Nicholle's chest. "An army. He said he has an army. Wills has to be stopped, Chris."

"But how? We're in no position to challenge him on anything."

"There's one way. The streets. Something he doesn't know much about."

chapter 11

"Whose body is it?"

"Some nurse found wired on pakz. She would've died anyway. We filtered the blood, flooded it with medinites, added lung capacity, and cardiovascular, muscular, and optical enhancements. So we've bloody given her a second chance. In a way."

The voices flickered across Thia's memory, barely registering as familiar. She knew these people, but their names escaped her, like a dream upon waking. When she opened her eyes, she did recognize them—Eyon Klé, the cyberneticist in the M31 Unit, and Dran Secobar, her boss. She was propped up in a bed, in a grey room with bright lights. Machinery lined the walls, manned by several white-coated lab assistants. Her bed was the only piece of furniture in the room. No chairs or tables.

"Ah, there she is. Hello, Thia," Eyon said. "Do you know who we are? Do you know who you are?"

He had monochrome face and hair—both tan—with a large forehead. His eyes drooped in the corners, giving him a constantly sad look.

"I-I—" Her voice halted. She wanted to ask why she was strapped to a bed and why she felt like she'd been strained through a cheese grater.

"I need to tweak the speech center."

"Is this going to work?" Dran said. His permanent scowl deepened, hardening his features, and narrowed eyes glinted as his lips puckered in disapproval. "The other ten were less than optimal."

"They were dead. This one was still alive," Eyon said, fiddling with some machinery. "We tried to erase all memories and traces of personality, but there may be some leakage. Of course, we won't be able to tell until she's fully conscious. There, she should be able to speak now. Thia?"

120

"What did you do to me, you brain-addled quack?"

"That's her, all right," Dran said.

"You were found dead in the northeast laboratory, so we added you to the consciousness transference subject study. You no doubt heard about the enhancements we made, but it may be a little while before you'll be able to use them."

"You put me in a pakz-addicted body? No wonder I feel like hell. This was the only one you could find?"

"It's been refurbished. We even built up muscle mass. There should be minimal adjustment. Well, except for your looks. You're a brunette now, black hair, brown eyes, pouty lips," Eyon said.

"Improvement if you ask me," Dran said. He winked.

Thia flexed her right arm, broke the restraining trap, and grabbed Dran's throat. Thia tightened her grip, feeling his larynx buckle. His face reddened as he struggled to remove her hand.

"Thia!" Eyon said. He motioned to two blue-coated men, who peeled her hand away and held her down.

Dran coughed, holding his neck. "That bitch is crazy, Eyon. Did you do a mental scan?"

"I relied on her last review."

"Yeah, well, things happen. Make sure she's sane before you let her loose. And I want a full report on my desk tomorrow morning." Dran hurried out the door.

Eyon gave her a one-sided frown as the men strapped her back down to the bed, this time with four straps for each arm. They had forgotten about her legs, she thought, but she would remain still for now, attempt to find out as much intelligence as she could.

"Do try and be a good girl, or you may wind up like the first ten," Eyon said.

"I thought they'd been dead."

"Yes, but they were reanimated. At least for a time. But when they didn't perform satisfactorily..." His voice trailed off, as if mentioning their fate would make it come to pass.

"Why was I brought back to life?"

"You're a valued agent."

"That's bull. There're plenty of good agents who could take over without having to spend billions on a third-generation prototype." She paused. "Hunh. I guess that's all I am now. Talk about messed up."

"Don't be silly. You're enhanced. Better than any agent we've got. Do you remember what happened when you, uh…?" His voice trailed off. Eyon waved the two men away, who walked back to their post and kept a wary eye on Thia.

Flashes of images raced in her mind—a laboratory, a room filled with various devices, a woman, a man—but they blurred together in a nonlinear manner, like scenes from a movie out of sequence.

"Not really."

"Do you remember your childhood?"

She tried to think backward, but the images fizzled as she tried to focus on them—glimmers of a dark-haired mother who yelled a lot. But that wasn't right. Or at least it didn't seem right.

"No. Vaguely. But not really. Like…it's someone else's memory."

"It may take time. Here. I'll give you something to sleep."

Before she could react, a wave of black washed over her.

✿

The voices again. No doubt Dran wanted to keep an eye on his investment. The fact she was conscious would probably go unnoticed for a few seconds. This time she kept her eyes closed. But…something was different.

"Yes, and you were right. Her original neurotransmitters exhibited aberrations. But they've been corrected."

"Good."

"She's conscious."

She opened her eyes, annoyed at their realization. Dran leaned down and spoke loudly in her ear.

"Thia, can you hear me?"

Dran was dressed in a different suit—grey with black pinstripes. She must've slept through the night.

"I can hear you perfectly. How are you today?"

"I'm fine. Strange of you to ask."

"Strange how?"

"Because the first thing out of your mouth is usually an insult. Or like yesterday when you choked me."

She remembered doing it, but she couldn't understand why.

"You're right, Mr. Secobar. I don't know why I did it. Do accept my apology."

"Are you kidding me? Since when do you apologize for anything? Or call me Mr. Secobar?"

"Since…" She tried to think back to the last time she did, but drew a blank. "I can't remember." And that was the truth. It had fleetingly occurred to her to lie. But why would she lie?

"That makes two of us." He turned to Eyon, hands on hips. "I thought you said she checked out."

"I said I corrected the aberrations on her brain cells."

"Hell, we need those aberrations back. She can't go prowling through back alleys shooting at the bad guys. She's more docile than a kindergarten teacher."

"I think kindergarten teachers have to be pretty tough, actually," Eyon said.

Dran closed his eyes, breathing deeply. "Never mind. Just get her back the way she was. I'll just wear a steel collar."

"You're the boss. I'm afraid I'll have to put you under again, Thia."

"That's all right, Doctor. Thank you for taking good care of me," she said.

Dran visibly shuddered. "See what I mean? The test phase is a bitch. And I want another report this afternoon."

✧

"Thia?"

Someone held an eye open, shining a bright light in it. She grabbed the arm that held the light and sat up.

"You keep shining that in my eye and I'll shove it up your ass."

"Ha! There she is. Good work, Doc," Dran said, grinning. He had on the same suit, which meant it was the same day, or two weeks later. She released Eyon's hand.

"I'm tired of the both of you poking and prodding me, asking dumb questions. When do I get out of here? And what the hell do I look like?"

"I'll get you a mirror," Eyon said. He stepped out of the room, leaving her with Dran. One side of his mouth curled up.

"What are you smiling at?" she said.

An apathetic look, deposited by facial drift, came over him, which meant he was excited, but didn't want to show it. This must be important, she thought. Whatever it was.

"I'll be straight with you. Wills Ryder is still behind on implementation of consciousness transference. We wanted to give him some slack, see what he came up with, then shut him down and take his data. But he's been shopping for information on cloning and looking to legalize it. He was holed up in his Fiji lab, but he went to Baltimore for a meeting with some industry execs."

Pounding heart, clammy skin. But she didn't know why. She fought it down while attempting to look nonchalant.

"If you know where he is, why do you need me?" she said.

"Because he disappeared, then the four executives were found dead around the state."

"That doesn't exactly follow." She recalled the name, Wills, and vaguely, the face, but there was definitely a connection. They had known each other somehow. But she couldn't remember.

"A source at the Port of Baltimore said a limo had pulled up to a warehouse. He got the license plate and we ran it. It was Ryder's. So we scanned the whole area and found traces of their DNA. Bold move."

"Too bold."

"Why do you say that?"

Why did she say that? "I—he's cautious. Usually. Unless there's something he really wants. Then he can be ruthless." How did she know that?

Eyon returned with a mirror, a small, silver affair. "Here you go." He undid the straps, casting furtive glances at her.

"Don't worry, Doc. I'm not going to bite," she said.

When her arms were free, Thia snatched the mirror from him. She sat up and regarded herself. Her hair was long, down to her waist, raven black. A change from her short, red locks. She'd either cut it or wear it up. All that hair hanging about scratched her skin like a rucksack.

Her eyes were large and brown, with barely visible lashes, but thick eyebrows. They had started to grow together, like a bridge between two islands. Her nose angled past the normal ending point, but it was not unattractive—merely an interesting anomaly. Dran had been right about the lips. Full, pouty, in an eternal pucker. The olive skin was flawless, as smooth as the fruit itself, plump and taut. Not like her previous ruddy skin.

"Interesting," she said.

"Ruthless, eh? What makes you say that?" Dran said.

"What?"

"Wills Ryder. You said he could be ruthless. I mean, you would know. You were lovers. I had sent you to him. Remember?"

That was it. Sketches of images danced across her mind. A deserted beach in Madagascar, a ski chalet in the Alps, a heated pool at the Hilton. An eternal promise. Revelation of subterfuge. Betrayal.

"Bastard. He even stole back the ring," she said.

"What ring?" Eyon said.

She hesitated. "Just a ruby ring I liked."

"An engagement ring?" Dran said.

"No," she lied.

"Good. Can't have my best agents running around with broken hearts. Makes for unstable relationships and unreliable intelligence."

Unreliable intelligence. If only they knew. She smiled in response, pushing the thoughts from her mind. Her memories were returning. But there was something different, something there that shouldn't be.

"This leakage, Doc. What characteristics can it take?" she said.

"Well, you may remember things that didn't happen to you, or you may recognize people you've never met. Smells or tastes may trigger memories that aren't there. We don't have much experience in this arena, so you'll be able to give us invaluable information," Eyon said.

"I'm not connected."

"We didn't want to introduce too much to your brain. Once we have you stabilized, you'll be connected."

It was weird, she thought, not being connected. Not being able to tap a finger and find what you wanted, call whom you wanted. She felt detached, isolated from the mainstream. Not in the know. Keeping tabs on her informants, her contacts, her field agents—it's what occupied her mind. Now there was just trying to piece together memories, for good or ill, even those that weren't hers.

And which was which? It was hard to tell, at least now, before her brain had a chance to sort through them all. Perhaps her dominant brain would push out the other memories, feelings, recollections—the ones that didn't belong. But she didn't hold out much hope for that. She was stuck in this body, unless this one was destroyed, and she doubted they could repeat the process. If they did, she'd be even less of herself. Someone else. An amalgamation of a pakz addict, herself, and probably some homeless bum who got kicked out by an ex-wife.

When she'd signed up for the agency, she certainly hadn't expected this.

"So when will I be stabilized?"

"Hopefully by tomorrow. We've got to get you in the field," Dran said. "If anyone can get Wills Ryder, it's you."

"Your other lackeys can't follow a lead?" she said.

"Not like you. So we'll let you out of bed to perform some tests on you. Strength, endurance, memory, stuff like that. Right, Doc?" He clapped Eyon on the back, who almost pitched forward onto the bed. When he righted, he cleared his throat.

"Yes, stuff like that, as it were."

"As a matter of fact, try to stand up," Dran said.

She threw off the sheet. A self-molding yellow plastic gown clung to her body. Swinging her legs off the bed, she found the annoying crackle in her knees gone.

"This is a younger body," she said. Even with the medinites in her old body, she still knew youth when she felt it.

"By ten years. Do you feel it?" Eyon said.

"Yes. Feels good." The cheese grater sensation had disappeared, replaced by a white-washed but newly energized feeling. Like a clean slate. *Almost.*

She stood, stretched. Definitely more limber. She feared to think what uses her flexibility had been put toward. Her muscles weren't developed as much as she'd like, but a few workouts in the gym would remedy that.

"So?" Dran said.

"I can definitely work with this," she said.

○

Her hair was braided and wrapped around her head, like some medieval German barmaid. She didn't know what else to do with it. Dran had bought her a navy pants suit that draped well. Her breasts were bigger, so the bulge in the center of her chest was a change. The buttons on her shirt strained. She was also shorter—an advantage for quickness, disadvantage for physical capacity. It would take some getting used to. Perhaps heels would help.

"I'm still not comfortable letting her go," Eyon said. He sulked on a loveseat in Dran's office. Dran sat behind his teak desk, swiveling in his chair from side to side, his fingertips in a diamond shape.

"Every moment that goes by is wasted. We need her out there," Dran said. "Besides, she thinks she's ready."

"I could use a couple of workouts, but I don't think this will call for strenuous exercise." She turned from the mirror and faced the two. "You want him alive, though, correct?"

"Yes," Dran said.

A shame, she thought.

Dran reached into the drawer and threw an envelope on the desk. "Here're your weapons and keys to a car. Your new identification has been processed through Social Security, so you're legit. Our contacts say Nicholle and her boyfriend visited a guy named Tuma, a mid-level gangster on the edge of town. Bowie, to be exact. She used to run pakz for him, back when she was on the street. They have a past. Bring her in, too."

"And the boyfriend?"

"You can kill him. I'm sure you'll enjoy that."

"Without a doubt." She snatched up the envelope.

"Which car?"

"Blue Octavian 250. And try not to wreck it."

Yeah, right.

chapter 12

"Welcome to Bowie" the sign read. Once a gleaming testament to a thriving enclave, now a rusted dent of metal that heralded a crime-ridden town bereft of public services.

Trash tumbleweeded down Annapolis Road on its way to the parking lots of abandoned stores. The burned hull of a bus sat atop a downed bus shelter, as if the driver failed to slow to pick up the passengers but instead mowed them under.

Nicholle would have felt more comfortable coming in daylight, but things being what they were, she had no choice.

The enclaves had been self-contained towns that grew food and provided jobs for those within. The area's answer to scarce gas and high prices. Anyone wanting to leave had to obtain authorization for extra gas. As a result, most family reunions, business deals, and friendly visits happened over wiho.

Then came high-efficiency batteries and fuel cells. People abandoned the enclaves for the purlieus. Lower income families filled in the gap, and when they began moving up and out, the criminal element moved in.

Tuma had the run of Bowie Town Center. You could get it all there. Pakz, skeemz, prostitutes, gambling. A local Las Vegas. Only without the one hundred-degree heat.

"You sure this is it?" Chris asked, dubiously.

"Yeah, I'm sure. Make a left here."

"Where are we going?"

"To see Tuma. He, ah, and she, heads up the Tets in this area."

"He and she?"

"Tuma's a dual-sexer. He can change at will, drawing up his well, you know. His breasts fold in. His face is effeminate, like a woman's, yet with a strong jaw, like a man's. When I first saw him—I call him 'him'—I didn't know what to think. I just kept staring at him, on the sly."

Thinking about him brought back memories. They used to talk long into the night together, sometimes as girlfriends, sometimes as more when he made the switch. It was weird, having your best friend and lover in the same person. He knew about women, from a personal perspective. Not exactly the typical pakz and skeemz dealer. But he was shrewd. Could sniff out a deal from fifty miles away. In a different reality, he could have been a corporate executive. Given Wills a run for his money.

Of course, he had looked at Nicholle as his ticket out, and treated her like that. She would get little extras and special attention, which pissed off some of the other rackers. Not that she cared what they thought, but when Tuma wasn't looking, they gave her hell.

She could only imagine what Tuma would do when he saw her. Maybe kill her on the spot. But this time, she was in a position to offer a stake in a legitimate company. Yeah, she was on the run from the Feds and dead broke, but he didn't have to know about the broke part.

"Where to?"

"Keep straight and make a left at the light."

Street lamps lined the road. But they stood silent and dark against the frame of night, victims of the shutdown in public services or vandalism. Even the traffic lights were dark.

Nicholle rolled down her window. The sound of drag-racing roared faintly in the distance, farther up 450. The road was pretty much a straight shot, perfect for the illegal sport. But racers took their life in their hands. No ambulances came out here.

They turned into the shopping plaza. A faded, battered yellow sign read "Welcome to Tuma's." Only "Tuma's" looked as if someone blowtorched the letters on a piece of metal and soldered it onto the existing sign that had read "Bowie Town Center."

The plaza was livelier than the main road. Cars filled the front part of the parking lot of the Great Goods building, where the prostitutes worked. Later on, any customer who found a parking space would be lucky. Neon lights lit up the darkness, firing pink and blue, like a disco muezzin, calling the faithful to party.

A large gate blocked the entrance to Tuma's, manned by five guards with guns. Snipers patrolled the roof of four of the buildings, walking back and forth, watching the people below. She'd seen them take out troublemakers with one bullet to the forehead. Military veterans who'd been shafted by the VA often found their way here. Money under the table, just to make ends meet.

"Where now?" Chris said.

"Pull into that bank down the street. Tuma's guards check all customers' bank accounts to see if they have money to spend. If not, they get beaten and sent on their way."

"So it doesn't help that our accounts are pachuta. And he's not likely to welcome you with a robe and ring like the prodigal son."

"That's where you come in."

"I knew that tightness in my chest was for a good reason."

Chris drove up a cracked, weed-infested driveway to a large brick building. The sign outside read "Adwele Bank," but had been graffitied with a gang symbol, the name "Mazebo," and the number 512. Mazebo had been killed a year ago, a casualty of a turf war.

"Fryer's in the trunk. Be right back," Chris said.

After retrieving the head gear, Chris slipped back into the seat beside her. "How much you want?"

"Fifty bill should do for now."

"Don't let 'em look too closely. I can match the versos on Bank Nigeria, but if you want the links, it'll take a while."

"They're not that thorough. Once they see the dollar signs, the green glow of cash should take us in."

Big rollers got deference to the infinity. That was one of the reasons Tuma'd been in the business so long—customer service. He had muscle working for him, cracking heads and collecting tibs, but Tuma himself focused on making the customers happy.

"Will they recognize you?" Chris said.

"Hard to say. He rotates the guards to prevent bribery. He could teach some things about business to CEOs." Regarding business *and* pleasure. The latter's what got him the seed money to take over Bowie Town Center. He paid off the few cops who had been caught out after the exodus. Bored and outnumbered, they succumbed to his monetary charms.

"Benefits, too?"

"If you can call a weekly visit to the cathouse a benefit."

"Works for me."

She hit him upside his head, but he had the fryer on.

"Just give me my money."

"Now you sound like a pimp. I feel so used," Chris said.

You don't know what used is, she thought. Nicholle turned toward the window. Trash blossomed from a dumpster, fat vines of plastic bags clinging to the sides. A fetid odor had drifted in with Chris. It had crept into her sinuses and signaled, "Welcome back."

"Okay, you've got fifty bill. I've got twenty-five." He slid off the fryer. "So we'll either be accepted with open arms or shot on sight."

"Let's hope it's not the latter," she said.

Chris started up the car and pulled out of the parking lot. They got in line behind the other cars and waited their turn at the gate.

"So this Tuma. He was your…"

His voice trailed off, leaving the missing words hanging in the air between them. What would Chris think of her if he knew the things she had done? She had to tell the truth, even if he would walk out on her.

"My supplier. Confidante. Pimp, of sorts. I was expected to 'be nice' to his best customers, but I could pick and choose. He never forced the issue, though. I could have refused."

"Did you?"

"Let's just say…" She paused. "I felt obligated."

"I see."

The tone in his voice spoke volumes. No, he didn't see, and he never would. If you hadn't been in the life, it was hard to explain. Probably a good thing.

"I'd take it all back if I could. After I ran out of money, I came home, did the twelve steps, found God, got a job, all that. Now all this happens and I'm back here where it started. If it weren't for the medinites, I'd probably be using again."

"We all make mistakes," Chris said. "At least you got yourself together. A lot of people can't say that. Believe me."

He sounded as if he'd seen the life reflected in someone he knew. A friend? Girlfriend? It was a conversation they would have to have later on. If they survived. Any thoughts beyond surviving the next ten minutes were a waste of energy.

"Now when we get in you're going to see some things you wish you hadn't, assuming we make it in alive." She offered up a silent prayer. "Just play along and act like you've seen it all your life."

"Like what kinds of things?"

"You'll see. Or maybe not. If he shoots us, you won't have to worry about it."

"Aren't we optimistic? I thought you found God. You could at least pray we make it in."

"I already did." But she wondered why she was just now getting around to it.

She slid on sunglasses. They pulled up to the gate and she rolled down the window. She remembered the guard's face, but not his name. Mo something or other.

Tuma lived at the other end of the plaza, inside Weisman's—or what used to be Weisman's, where one used to be able to find everything from automatic ovens to robot receptionists. From last she remembered, there were still a few left in the basement.

"You feemin'?" the guard said.

"Naw, we're clean. Heard about this place from a friend and thought we'd check it out. Might be lookin' to make an investment. Looks like you could use a spit shine," Nicholle said.

The smaller stores lining the road sat empty, dark, the purview of skeemz programmers who languished in sealed-off doorways—old black-and-white magfields that sputtered open and shut, their solar cells deteriorated. Strobe-light scenes of dust-covered merchandise and animatronic mannequins still lurching in torn, grey rags flickered by.

The evergreen tree in the middle of the plaza had grown since she last saw it; its upper branches had escaped the decaying Christmas ornaments and pakz wrappers that festooned the tree. A soft glow emanated from under layers of branches and strings of miniature Santas and snowmen that were missing limbs and heads. A life-size Mrs. Claus winked from an empty eye socket. She was clad in fishnet stockings and a metal bustier. A cat o' nine tails dangled from her upraised hand. An elf dressed in a gimp outfit knelt at her feet.

A gold lamé brassiere with green tassels was strung across Rudolph's antlers. On Rudolph's back was a naked elf, holding reins of barbed wire.

"This is sick," Chris whispered. Nicholle smiled, noting they had updated Rudolph's bra. The prostitutes had raided their underwear drawers to help decorate the scene for opening night, or so the story went.

Another gate blocked the entrance to Weisman's, manned by five guards. This was it, where they would either be shot or welcomed inside. Tightness swirled in her chest. She finally remembered the guard's name. Mozee. Short, built, with sloping shoulders and a downturned mouth to match. Zee for short. The Chinese had stepped up trade with Africa, and joint offspring often found their way to the States. Many of the gang members were mixed and called themselves Maros.

Three of the guards approached, guns bent sinister. She put her hand on Chris's knee to help calm him and reassure herself. Zee stood by the driver's side. A sec-drone flew inside and scanned them, then flew out and flashed an image for the guard. The bank versos blinked, along with their names and pictures.

"I don't believe it," Zee said, in a Kenyan lilt.

He bent down to look in the car. "You got *kobbads* of brass, Nicholle, comin' up in here. You expect to jes walk in and see Tuma?"

"I just want to talk, Zee. That's all. I brought something for him. Something he'll want."

"What?"

"Couple of bill."

"You think he need money?"

"What about you?"

"I got a tib on the side."

"You know what he wants, Zee. And I can offer that." On conditions that Zee didn't have to know about. "You want Tuma to know he could've had it but lost it because of you?"

Zee reached through the window, past Chris, and grabbed Nicholle by the shoulders. She screamed and lurched back.

"You think you can tell me what Tuma want? Bitch!"

He tried to pull her through the opening, but she latched onto the steering wheel and wedged her knees against it.

"Stop!" Chris said. He bit Zee's arm. Zee yelled, letting go of Nicholle. He punched Chris in the face. Zee opened the door and yanked her out. She fell onto the ground and looked up at him towering over her, gun drawn and pointed at her head.

She tapped her finger and whispered, "Call Tuma." He had probably blocked her calls, as she had his, but it was worth a try. Maybe he still had feelings for her. Or the desire for legitimacy. *Maybe.*

Zee grabbed her up and threw her on the hood of the car. Shards of pain radiated up her spine and down her legs. She opened her mouth, but only managed a raw gurgle.

"Don't you touch her!" Chris said, trying to scramble out of the car.

A ringing echoed in her head, but she didn't know whether it was a cog or the pain. A hand clutched her hair and dragged her off the hood and across the ground, scraping off the skin on her arm. She reached up and grabbed the hand. It brought her up, face to face with Zee.

"First I'm going to beat you, then I'm going to shoot you." He trained a gun on her face. The other guards held Chris at bay. Blood trickled out his nose and over his lips. All he had done was try to protect her, and he was being punished for it. She regretted having brought him into the whole sorry mess.

"Nicholle."

Tuma. He had picked up.

"Tuma. I'm outside with Zee. There's a slight misunderstanding. He says he wants to kill me. Now I think that would be a tragic loss. Don't you?"

"Liar! You're not talking to Tuma," Zee said.

"Well, I think you should wait to find out before making an irreversible decision," Nicholle said.

Zee hesitated, snarling. His teeth shone white behind his snarl, a slice of dazzling brilliance.

Tuma chuckled in her ear. "Yes, a slight misunderstanding. So after all this time, what brings you here?"

"Get Zee off me and I'll help you."

"Help me? What makes you think you can help me? And what do you want in return?"

"Look, Tu. Just give me ten minutes' face time. That's all. If you don't like what I'm saying, I'll be on my way."

"You walked out on me, Nick."

Nicholle bit her lip. "Let me explain in person."

"Five minutes."

The call ended. The gate started to open, which seemed to surprise the guards.

"Let her through," Tuma's voice announced on an old intercom. Zee's eyes narrowed. He snarled one last time and released his grip on her.

"Been a pleasure, Zee. Like old times," Nicholle said. She untangled herself from Zee and got in the car.

"Thank you," she whispered, wondering if her prayer had made it up through the chaos. They drove through the gate and parked in front of Weisman's. She gave Chris a guided tour to help keep her anxiety at bay.

"Drugs are in the basement, gambling on the first floor. Tuma's apartment and...other stuff is on the third. I'm going to tell him you can write skeemz. Know anything about that?"

"A little," Chris said.

"Good. If you don't know it, make something up. They're always looking for something new, like the Greeks."

"Greeks?"

"In the Bible, when Paul went to preach in Athens, it was said they were always looking for the latest thing."

"A piece of advice. Try not to use obscure biblical references with Tuma. You'll probably just piss him off."

"You don't even know Tuma."

Chris looked at the naked women dancing next to the slot machines on display in the window.

"Just a hunch," he said.

The doors opened onto a huge casino. People sitting on stools lined the front of the store, their right arms jerking an unseen handle. Their consciousness and bank accounts were connected directly to the House. Play until you ran out of money. Or passed out.

Along the side wall were the mechanical machines where one actually inserted coins. Two elderly men were playing those. Their arm movements were slower than the wiho gamblers, who didn't need to reach for coins. Topless women and bottomless men crossed the floor, bearing drinks. A garish red, gold, and green rug tied the room together in a nauseating style.

People from all walks of life—or so it seemed—crowded the game tables. Exec types, trap rats, pros, housewives, alkies, pimps, users. Tuma didn't care. As long as they had a black bottom line and behaved themselves, they were welcome. Some had been customers for years, working for what they could spend there.

They made a left at the craps table and walked up the escalator. The thing hadn't worked in years. At the top, a guard scanned them for weapons, then motioned them to a pair of double wooden doors. She steeled herself as she took hold of the glass knobs and opened the doors.

A Great Dane chased a naked woman past the doorway, almost bowling Nicholle over. Several people in the right corner lay naked on large pillows, limbs intertwined as they undulated to rhythmic gasps and moans. The dog jumped on the woman, knocking her to the ground. She giggled in delight.

A statue of King David stood in an alcove in silent witness. *Poor David.* Quite a different setting than what his holographic counterpart had. She wondered if she would see her museum again.

A large chandelier, hung with crystals, glowed with a low light in the middle of the room. Tuma sat on a red chaise lounge against the far wall, attended by barely clad women. He was in his male form. His eyes shone orange with diagonal slits for pupils. A mop of purple hair hung across his forehead and swept down his back. His skin had a sallow, yellow tone, which Nicholle feared would look even more yellow in brighter light. She approached him, undaunted by his changed appearance. A slender, forked tongue licked out, toward Nicholle. She drew back in surprise.

"Hello, Tuma. You've changed."

"For the better?" His voice was smooth, sounding both male and female, with the ability to enrapture listeners.

"Depends on your point of view. The tongue is definitely an advantage, though," she said.

A throaty laugh escaped Tuma, causing his attendants to smile. Sharpened canines glistened. Tuma arose and walked toward her, all six feet five inches of him. He walked like a ballet dancer, graceful for his height. Tight black leather pants and a shirt opened to the waist with a gun stuffed down the front. She wondered if the slit eyes were permanent, but nothing was quite permanent with Tuma. He went through phases, reinventing himself according to the current fashion trends. When she had left him, he'd been in a superhero stage. An overlay of bulky muscles shimmered over his skin, a cape attached to his bare shoulders. Nicholle hadn't minded the muscles, but the cape had kept getting in the way.

He circled her now, his tongue flicking over her face. She tried not to flinch.

"It's funny what I can sense with this tongue. Blood pressure, temperature, heart rate. Our friend the snake seems to have an inborn lie detector, at least with some enhancements. So…why are you here?"

Nicholle froze. The swirl in her chest tensed, coiling around her lungs. Two guards flanked Chris, sandwiching him between bulging muscles.

"Like I said, I can help you. Legitimacy. It's what you've always wanted." She could do it, if she had control of her company, but it'd be difficult. Difficult to get her company back, difficult to legitimize prostitution and drug use. Perhaps a reverse corporate residency in Las Vegas. Anything went there. She'd have to consult with the legal department, once she hired new attorneys. There'd be a housecleaning when she got back.

Think positive. Not if. When.

"Just like that?" His tongue licked at her ear, which was strangely erotic, strangely repulsive.

The purple of his hair evoked the scent of lavender; it misted the back of her throat. Fragrance enhanced. She coughed.

"Well, I'd have to consult—"

He cut her off. "Why'd you leave?" The hollow of his neck deepened as his neck muscles stiffened. He towered over her, pressing against her shoulder. This was the crux of the matter, why she left.

"I was taking off the top to pay for my skeemz habit. Krank found out and blackmailed me. But he kept wanting more and more. I was afraid to come to you, and it all finally came crashing down. My brother had blocked my accounts. I owed more than I had, so I went to Wills. He said he'd give me the money if I came in. So I did. Went through detox. Got clean, got a job. Some stuff happened. And here I am."

"I told Krank to blackmail you."

His words hit her like raw electricity.

"You did what?"

"I wanted to test you. See how far you'd go in stealing from me."

She should've known. Gangsters like Tuma didn't stay in business long without knowing who had their hand in the till. Which could be anybody.

"So *you* drove me away."

"Oh, don't blame me for your habit. I was just a dumb *bozi* to you."

"It wasn't like that."

She hadn't wanted the addiction. It had been all part of 'the life.' The need to belong drove her to that first hit, that first trip into perfect skeemz reality where wishes were Beemers and everyone rode. Rode the avalanche of kaleidoscopic colors that bent around your inhibitions and detoured suppressed secrets, honing in on harbored desires and suppressed neuron firings. Psychotropic euphoria.

"I guess you were just another addict."

That hurt. As much as she had done for him. "I was a loyal racker who brought in a hundred k a night and who saved your ass from Lydo. You'd be skinned alive in some back alley pakz house if it weren't for me."

"Don't flatter yourself." He clicked his thumb and pinky nails together. Things were looking up.

"What I want is respect for my contributions."

"I thought you wanted help," Tuma said.

"I deserve both," she said.

"Cocky, aren't we?"

"You used to like that."

"Times change."

"But people rarely do. The fact that one of your minions hasn't killed me yet tells me you want something. Something other than what I'm offering."

Tuma tensed, his jaw muscles flexing. Whenever he wanted something badly, he would click his nails together, and tonight they'd been going like a dominatrix's whip on a politician's back.

"You always were clever." He drew out the last word like a piece of taffy, as if savoring the sound on his lips.

"Maybe we can work something out."

"Maybe you can give me a bill and I'll think about it."

Ribbons of queasiness fluttered in her chest and a sensation of weightlessness came over her. She would have to lie her way out of that one.

"Tuma. The company's going through hard times right now. Most of my cash is tied up in investments. I can't float a bill…yet. Soon, though." She'd be more than happy to forfeit that, and more, if she could get her father back, her company back, out of the clutches of her brother. *Brothers.*

"Wait until when?"

"Until—"

"Until you clear your name with the Feds?"

"So. Been keeping up, eh?"

"Yeah, I watch the news now. Mostly to check on my stock. Couldn't help but notice your face burnt to the verso. Tsk, tsk. Embezzling money." He lifted a slender finger and waggled it back and forth.

"It wasn't me. Wills embezzled the money and left town."

"Oh, yes. I heard he was on the run, too. Must run in the family."

Red flashed across her vision. She reached out and grabbed Tuma's gun in the front of his pants. She pressed the weapon to his face. The two guards left Chris's side and stepped forward.

"Back off! Or the back of his head gets a hole," Nicholle said.

The guards did as they were told. Tuma began to chuckle.

"Now you're going to kill me?" he said.

"I just want to talk."

"We've been talking."

"No, we've been bullshitting." Nicholle forced him over to the chaise lounge and ran her hand along the wood to feel for the button. Top right, under the trim.

The latch to the door behind the chaise clicked open. A shaft of light scalened the floor. She pressed the weapon in Tuma's throat in the direction of the door, pushing him backward. Once through, she closed and locked the door behind them and retracted the gun.

"Sit down," she said, motioning toward the swing. Tuma's sex dungeon resembled a Torquemada confessional room, replete with cages, spanking horses, bondage tables, whipping racks, slings, bars, and a table spread with catheters, enema equipment, and neck braces—tools of a medical fetish.

She took up a seat on a bondage table, brushing aside the leather straps. This part of his life she had avoided as much as she could. Pain was not her thing. She hadn't minded the body sling, though. It had reminded her—in a weird, dark sort of way—of the hammock in her grandmother's back yard.

Oma.

"What?" she said.

"I didn't say anything."

"I thought I heard—. Never mind." Must've been her nerves, she thought. "So what is it you want me to do?"

"You remember Lydo."

"Of course."

Tuma's eternal thorn in the side. Lydo led a squad of skeemz writers and rackers on the other side of Baltimore, in Owings Mills. They worked out of the basement of the mall. Nothing like Tuma's operation, though. They were connected. Really connected. His programmers just sat, wearing fryers, writing skeemz for weeks at a time, their medinites monitoring and patching the effects of inactivity, nourishment forced into them intravenously. They looked like hollowed-out corpses, skin and flesh sagging on their bones, but man, the end product seemed worth it. *Groundbreaking, visionary shit.* Everyone wanted a Lydo skeemz. Best in the business.

"What about him?"

"He's working on something new. Rumors, yeah, but rumors with teeth and a tail. Rumors I don't want bitin' me in the ass down the road."

Tuma's business had already taken a hit from Lydo's skeemz. Why risk disease and even death if you could have a virtual prostitute? Sure, some still liked the danger element of live action, but as skeemz got more sophisticated, more chose to partake.

"So what do you want me to do? Get it from the horse's mouth, then shut it down?"

"As I said, clever. Should be easy with your skeemz guy. They're always looking for the latest and greatest."

"Funny, I said the same about you," she said.

"Apparently they're more choosy than I am. If your skeemzer's on drugs, they won't take him."

"Don't worry."

"Is that all he is to you? Just a programmer?"

His words took her aback. Sure, they had been lovers, but they always compared notes on other conquests. There wasn't jealousy between them, at least not before now.

"You're...concerned about my relationship with Chris?"

"Don't flatter yourself. You weren't that good."

"But better than most. That's neither here nor there, though." She switched gears, changing the subject, trying to avoid confrontation. "So how do we get in? Just show up on his doorstep and ring the bell?"

"That's one way. The other way takes a bit of time, though."

She thought of her father, languishing in the hospital, about to be euthanized. "Time is something I don't have."

"What do you mean?"

She contemplated whether to tell him about her father, Wills, Perim, the company. They had been through thick and thin together, for a while, and he had given her advice in the past. But if there was one thing she had learned, it was not to put all your cards on the table unless you were out of options. So she decided just to tell him about her father.

"Shit. I mean, what a sac job. Uh, I mean, sorry."

"It's all right. I know what you meant."

Tuma started playing with the ring on his left hand, a silver skull biting a dead rat. The rat hung limp between a set of sharpened teeth, blood trickling out in a thin ruby stream, courtesy of solar nanites. He pulled it part way off, then twisted it round and round with his pinky. The skull spun around like an amusement ride, the rat along for the thrill.

"So if I do this for you, you'll help me?"

"Anything." His full lips spread into a crescent, but the effort left his eyes untouched.

"Two things," she said.

"What?"

"First, a mill each, nonnegotiable."

"That all?" Sarcasm blanketed his voice. "And the other?"

"A sepsis."

"What kind?"

"As you said, the latest and greatest. Something Lydo's never seen before, no countermeasures."

"That can be arranged," Tuma said. "Anything else?"

"Yeah, but I'll explain later. Still need to work out a few details."

He stood up and walked over to where she sat, his body a serpentine arc, gliding as he went. The slow, sinuous movements conveyed dominance and sensuality, the things she remembered most about him. He lifted his hand to her cheek and traced the outline, then paused at her jaw, his palm hovering underneath.

"Ah, the coy Nicholle." He leaned in close, putting his weight against the edge of the table, between her legs, brushing his lips against her ear. "I missed that," he whispered. Hot, shallow gasps fluttered down the length of her neck, tickling the hair on her nape. She had to restrain from hunching her shoulders to dispel the tickling sensation.

"Remember when we used to stay in bed all day?" he said.

"Unforgettable." She tried to sound convincing by catching the sound in the back of her throat, the words barely escaping her lips. Her drug trips were a giddy collection of colors, sounds, and tastes, more so than usual. She barely remembered Tuma during those episodes, never mind any movement beyond lolling her head from side to side.

She leaned back, brought one leg across, and slid off the table, leaving the gun. Now pressed against Tuma, the musky scent of Q3 cologne triggered her flirtatious sensibilities, but she dampened them. There were, however, tendrils of a different scent. Something…off-kilter.

She lifted her chin and placed it on the edge of his shoulder.

"It's late. I'm going to get some rest before we go to Lydo's."

He hung his head as a measure of breath escaped his nostrils. "Your room's as you left it," he said in a low voice.

She froze. After all this time. Then she knew. The off-kilter scent. The sickly yellow wasn't a fashion statement, it was a medical statement. He was ill. He'd never admit it, of course. Any sign of weakness in a crime lord was a death sentence, but his outrageous fashion was more than a statement now. It was a camouflage. She squeezed his arm.

"When I get back, anything you need, it's yours," she said. Outlaws didn't generally have medinites, as they were monitored by a service that could be subpoenaed.

His mouth set in a grim line, and he nodded his head. He walked over to the table and retrieved the gun. Fingering it, he spoke his plan.

"For the record, I wrestled the gun away and forced you to do this."

"Any way you want it," she said.

He raised the gun and waved her toward the door. When she emerged on the other side, Chris was cinched up even tighter by the two guards, as if they were waiting for Tuma's body to be shoved out the door at them, whereupon they would exact their revenge on Chris.

"Escort our guests to her old room in the basement," Tuma said. "She'll be leaving in the morning."

"You mean we," Nicholle said.

"Hostage."

Her heart sank. She should've guessed. He didn't extend trust too far, especially to ex-thieves.

The guards shoved Chris toward the double doors and they flew open when he stumbled through the doorway. She and the two guards followed.

Nicholle shuddered at the thought of the basement. It had been more than a year and at times she still woke up drenched in sweat after nightmares about the place. She caught up to Chris and they walked in silence down both escalators. Each step echoed in her head, a steady reminder of what she was about to confront.

"Don't go sabucci down there," she said.

"You already told me."

A flash of agony poked her mind. "A reminder never hurts."

They turned past the gamblers on the first floor, the sounds of coins clinking and dealers calling for last bets filling the air. She recalled trudging up the stairs many nights, grateful for the sounds of mirth, happy that a world of hope still existed. Of course, that had been after a bad trip, but those had started coming more often just before she left. No matter how hard she tried to customize a skeemz, the trips kept getting worse and worse, which didn't happen to other people. They went along their merry, trippy way, paying obeisance and funds to Tuma and receiving their due recompense.

The unmoving escalator descended into an ebony pit. Raw fear stroked her inward being. Her pulpy hands wrung together. She bit her lip. Flashes of color strobed the darkness, feeding the monochrome hunger of the basement residents. Pulsating music beat in time to the flashes, sending vibrations through her body. Nicholle paused when she reached the bottom, letting her eyes become accustomed to the dimness. It might have changed since she last saw it, but she doubted it.

The bottom of the steps opened to a cavernous room. The skeemz users sat lining the walls, immersed in their programming. Pakz users were more unpredictable. Some roamed the floor, some jumped and shouted, some sat quietly. In the distance, screams of ecstasy and agony pierced the dark.

A moldy smell blanketed the room, underlying all else. Even the acrid smell of the drugs the pakz users smoked or sniffed was overpowered by the musty odor.

A thin outline of a large serpent moved across the floor and curled up a column. Chris jumped back when he saw it. She'd done the same thing when she first arrived. The guards shoved them through the hologram. Spying the door to her room, she hooked Chris's arm and took off across the floor, avoiding the roaming users who screamed at whatever demon floated into their line of sight. She motioned to the guards that he was with her and it was all right.

And Tuma was right. The room was as she'd left it. Long and narrow, painted pink. Multicolored curlicues twisted on the ceiling, moving in rhythm to whatever beat pounded the airwaves. A Yebedor print hung on the wall over the single bed. *Woman With Curves.* A small refrigerator stood in the corner on the floor. She feared to look at what was inside.

"Quaint," Chris said.

"Thanks. Home away from home." Quite different from a four-poster king-sized bed, but the mattress was good. She'd been happy on more than a few occasions to fall into that bed.

He held out a hand. She took his arms instead, leaning on his chest until they were wrapped firmly around. Ensconced.

"So what now?" he said.

"I have to go to a rival of Tuma's and find out what new skeemz he has. Shut him down. He lives north of Baltimore in Owings Mills. Name of Lydo."

Chris reared back. His hands cupped her shoulders. "Are you crazy? You could get killed. The hell does he want you to go there for?"

"Relax, I've been there before. I'll just make him think Tuma and I are still on the outs and I'm looking to make some money on the side since I'm on the run. I had some connections back then, trading channels. If he thinks I'm there to turn on Tuma, he'll probably welcome me with open arms. Piece of cake," she said.

"I saw a movie once where that tactic didn't work."

"Probably, but I don't have much of a choice."

Chris edged closer, until her forehead touched his chin. He wrapped his arms around her, enfolding her in the cradle of his chest.

"Stay the night. You need your rest," he said.

"I can't. The sooner I go, the better. My father doesn't have much time."

She wished she could have stayed in Chris's arms all night. Pop a skeemz where reality didn't matter. Didn't exist.

"Then stay an hour."

"All right."

chapter 13

Nicholle pulled up to Owings Mills Mall, high beams on, since the building and parking lot were pitch black. It was Lydo's ploy, to make it seem as if no one was there. Guard towers ringed the mall, connected with a barbed wire fence.

She pulled up to the fence and spoke into a speaker box posted on a rusted metal pole.

"Nicholle Ryder to see Lydo. I have a business proposition for him."

She wasn't sure if she'd be let in on that thin line, but when the gate began to creak open, she was pleasantly surprised. After she parked outside the main entrance, she walked up and old-fashioned doors slid open.

The smell of sweat and musty air accosted her nostrils. An alarm sounded throughout the hall. A shrill wail. Lights blinked. The sound of booted steps pounded off the walls, shaking the floor. She spun around to go back the way she came, but the doors wouldn't open.

She twisted around to see the boots' owners. Toothless open-mouthed faces stared back at her. Tubes ran from the backs of their throats and hung, limp, by their waists, dripping white liquid, as if they'd just been ripped from the source. Their eyes were covered in wraparound sunglasses. A blackened hole took the place of a tongue and teeth. Enlarged veins throbbed along the sides of the hole. The lips had atrophied—desiccated flesh that would peel away and fall off at any moment. A zig-zag of circuit boards rose like a city skyline on top of their heads, hairless flesh ending in slotted data.

The guards didn't speak, but stepped to the side and pointed their weapons in the direction she was to go. She edged around them and cautiously took the lead.

They all stepped into a green glass elevator and one of the leech mouths pushed the button for the top floor. As the elevator rose, the layout of the building could be seen through the glass—a long hallway with dilapidated stores lining the corridor. Dirty pock-marked green marble tile covered the floor. In some places, chunks of marble were missing, revealing grey stone underneath. The exterior windows were blacked out.

A few storefronts were lit, illuminating guards walking about, carrying weapons. Strewn about were several mannequins, some charred, some missing limbs. The scene disappeared and the next one arose as the elevator climbed. Second floor. Better lighting. Drug-using customers staggered between store stalls, sampling the wares. One-stop shopping.

They rose to the third floor and the doors opened. Two more guards approached—human looking—and stopped in front of her. No one spoke. They must have communicated directly with one another. No need for speech. The end of a weapon jabbed her in the back and propelled her forward. She tripped and fell. One of the guards grabbed her up. She hobbled off the elevator and headed for the large glass door.

"Stop, Ms. Ryder. You will be interrogated in the Pea Pod."

It wasn't the words that stopped her, it was the tone. It rose and fell haphazardly, like the robots in old two-dimensional movies, as if the speaker wasn't used to participating in conversation. Maybe Lydo's empire was crumbling, she thought. Or maybe he was taking funds from maintenance and putting them in research and development. And what did interrogation consist of? Thumb screws and bamboo shoots? Or a truth skeemz?

"Interrogated for what?" she said. No answer.

The guard prodded her down the hall to a storefront that was the most lit of the gaping holes that lined the corridor. A path was swept in the middle of the debris that littered the floor—broken glass, dirty clothes, empty pakz.

She was forced along to the back where a row of barber chairs stood. A small stand sat by each chair, filled with knives, wires, chips, and pakz.

Thoughts raced, her mind jumbling sentences, images—too fast to register—a montage of pain and addiction. She braced herself, stiffening her limbs.

"No." She shook her head. "No!" The guards lifted her by the arms and shoved her in one of the chairs. Straps circled her head, chest, and legs, pinning her down. Fear fired through her mind.

"What the hell are you doing? I have a business proposition for Lydo. I demand to see him!"

"In time," came the reply. A disembodied voice, coming, it seemed, from the walls themselves—a voice that was beyond familiar. Lydo's.

"Lydo! Listen to me! You want Tuma gone, right? I can help you."

No reply. The guard picked up a pakz and stuck it to her arm. She tried to squirm as the ultrasonic waves opened her pores, but her arm was held fast. A cool spray of drugs entered her skin and suddenly all was right with the world. Peace and light suffused the air. Colors appeared. Hues of pink, orange, and blue swirled and coalesced, making a path beneath her feet. She wanted to step on the path and ride the colors. But something pecked at the back of her mind. This shouldn't be happening. The pakz should have no effect on her. Her medinites should negate the effects, bleach out the colors. But if anyone could get her addicted again, it'd be Lydo. He must have reprogrammed her medinites, switched off the pakz block.

The straps that held her retracted, freeing her. The colored path beckoned, its mesmerizing hues bending and twisting as they spelled her name. She fell out of the chair and onto her knees.

"The medinites...block...drugs..." she stammered.

"Oh, they normally would." The voice was close. His voice. "But Tuma gave me your code."

The words resounded, echoing in her head as they bounced from left brain to right. *Good.* The floor contracted and flung itself from her. She jerked as she tried to grasp something to keep from falling. But then the floor returned to give her balance.

Part of the plan, but still, she couldn't succumb. She had to pick the right time. So she didn't step on the rainbow path, on the tangerine road to the emerald city. She envisioned a dark room, with herself crouching in the corner.

"You've changed, Nicholle. Usually you'd be dancing the pas de deux from Swan Lake by now. At least that's what Tuma told me. He also told me you'd try to pull something like this. He doesn't want a war.

"But perhaps you've built up a resistance. How about my latest skeemz? I got the idea after visiting a shaman in Peru. It's supposed to drive out your inner demons. Manny, fry up the latest for Ms. Ryder."

In an instant, the darkened storefront faded and she was in a hot, crowded room that smelled of herbs and sweat. The humidity stifled her, plastering a wet stickiness on her. Various masks decorated the wood-paneled walls.

She was sitting on a crude wooden floor, in a circle with ten other people. They all looked like typical backpackers—young, Bohemian, fresh-faced, enthusiastic. The shaman, what she assumed was the shaman, was a short, thin man who wore a colorful robe and a knit hat with large hanging tassels. He stared at Nicholle. His eyes a black that drew one into an emptiness.

"I'm glad you could join us," he said. "It's the start of an important journey you must take."

"Riiight," she said. She clapped her hands twice to get the exit menu, but nothing happened. The other participants stared at her with the same empty eyes.

One said, "You must stay."

Nicholle clapped her hands again. Still nothing. Lydo had disabled the exit menu. She was in it until the end.

The shaman passed around ten wooden mugs, then held up a container.

"I will pour out the amount you must drink." He got up and poured some in everyone's cup. When he reached Nicholle, who was last, he handed her the jug.

"You drink this," he said. She took the jug and sniffed the contents. A vile odor seeped up.

"Ugh. You've got to be kidding. I'm not drinking that." She set the jug down and pushed it away. The sound of a plasma gun initiating filled the air.

She turned and was greeted with the incongruous sight of a man dripping in tassels holding an ES47 lason rifle, trained on her head.

"Drink." His voice was calm, almost inviting. She retrieved the jug from the middle of the floor, held her breath, and brought it to her lips. The liquid inside was a murky brown. She could only guess what was in it. She opened her mouth, tipped the offensive liquid in and swallowed.

"Chug, chug, chug!" the others chanted. The stuff tasted as bad as it smelled. She had to give Lydo recognition, though. This skeemz made reality seem fake. Smells, tastes, and sounds—all enhanced to a point of superhuman ability. If he just made it pleasurable, he'd have a trillion-dollar seller on his hands.

When she finished, she threw the jug across the room. It stopped in mid-air. *Kink in the program?* The others cheered. Then their cheers slowed and faded. The room tilted and contracted, skewing the view, elongating faces.

Then blackness. Silence. *Thank goodness.* But where was everyone?

"Hello?" she called. "Hello?"

A small voice sang in the distance. "It's a cookin'. It's a comin'. It's a cookin'. It's a comin'."

Wha?

Her mother used to sing that to her when she was cooking something for Nicholle. The telescopic image of a little girl came into view, which widened to show her in a room surrounded by dolls. The little girl was her. She was singing to her dolls as she used one hand to prepare water and grass for them to eat. Suddenly her parents' voices boomed from the other room.

"I can't believe you're cheating on me again! I told you to get rid of your whore!"

"You knew what you were getting coming into this."

The scene darkened. Her head whirled as voices spoke.

"Got the latest right here. This Asia Blue pakz will make you feel like you the fema."

A drain opened beneath her and she circled around and around. Great bats circled with her, hissing as they went, spewing fire. She screamed and ducked, trying to avoid the flames. Other screams joined hers, shrieks of horrific anguish, as if coming from hell itself. She caught the edge of the drain and clung to it. Her legs battered the walls of the drain as the force of winds pounded. A bat hissed, spitting flames on her hands. The heat blistered her fingers and she let go. She fell down the drain, toward the screams. *Damn, Lydo. This shit is beyond real.*

Now.

She accessed the source code using the commands Chris gave her. A phalanx of numbers and symbols scrolled down her vision. She waited for the correct sequence. *Still falling.* She tuned out the external, concentrated on what was in front of her, even as she turned end over end. *Not much time.* The lines of code a vague recollection. She didn't know why. She was an artist, not a wihead. But no mistaking—there were programs for communications, skeemz, purchasing, R&D. Seemed Lydo ran a tight ship. No wonder he had the game on lockdown.

There. She uploaded the sepsis between the data declarations and the functions. It glowed blue for a split second, then took on the orange of the scrolling code.

The low hum she heard when she first arrived ceased. She stopped falling. The lights dimmed, then went out. Flooded in black. *It worked.* She stood up, trying to remember where she was.

Third floor. Down the hall.

But how would she get out? Not even the light from a panel to guide her. She dragged her feet along to avoid stepping on something sharp, pushing debris to the side. Mentally laid out the map of the mall. She was by the Pea Pod. *Escalator to the right.*

She held out her arms, waving them in front of her. Primitive radar. She made it to the door after stumbling over mannequin parts. Then the lights came on. Lydo stood in front of her. She stepped back, shocked. Tuma had told her the sepsis would wipe out the entire system. Even the backup.

"Nice try. I'll give you that," Lydo said. He held a gun on her, trained on her heart.

It pounded. *Thanks for nothing, Tuma.* "Lydo, look—"

"Shut up. Wills told me to chill your shit. Sorry, ba—"

The lights blinked out. For good this time, she hoped. She dropped to the floor, wondering what the hell Wills was doing talking to Lydo, but she didn't have long to sit and contemplate. Blue flared above her. In the half-second of light, she found Lydo's knee and rammed her heel in it. He fell; the gun clattered across the floor. She took off, right, then slowed, feeling for the escalator. Heat seared. She pitched forward and fell. The sharp edges of the steps cut into her as she rolled down, over and over.

She landed in a heap at the bottom, open wounds bleeding warm.

A dark figure moved on the floor above. She strained to get up. Ran down the hall and turned into a storefront. Footsteps followed. *Damn.* Her foot hit something and it slid on the floor. She bent down, felt for it. An arm. Plastic. She picked it up and stood by the entrance. Her eyes adjusted to the dark. The figure approached, slowly, gun at shoulder height. She eased down and felt for something small. A gambling chip. Some people still carried them around, even in this day and age. She threw it farther into the store to draw him in. He took the bait. Stepped inside. The arm made a sickening crack on the back of his head. He fell to the floor. Nicholle pried the gun from his hand and hurried toward the escalator.

✿

She slept soundly on the trip back and awoke to Mozee banging on her window. She wiped the drool from the seat and her mouth and opened the window.

"Aww, Sleeping Beauty's back," he said.

"No, I'm Snow White and you're Grumpy," she said.

He reached in an arm, grabbed her by her shirt, and shook her. Her head snapped back and forth like a wihead on a bad skeemz.

"Zee!" someone shouted.

He gave her one last shake. Kicked the car door as she drove through the open gate.

"You need Jesus, Zee!" she yelled out the car window. He ran after her and kicked the trunk. She sped up, smiling at him in the rearview.

✿

They sat in the food court at a dust covered table. Chris had long ago lost the tie and jacket. He sat, sullen looking, in a sweat stained button-down shirt open at the collar and sleeves. Tuma sank back in his chair, his self-assuredness cast aside like last year's accessories line.

"Lydo's is shut down, for now anyway. I don't know how long—" Nicholle started.

"I had a team there waiting for security to go down," Tuma said. "They've already taken over. I decided it's what I wanted. I've been in the business too long for legitimacy. Plus…"

He left off, all of them knowing with what to fill in the blank: Cancer.

Tuma continued, despite the leaden pause. "I have something else. Wills came to me, looking for techrus. Said it was high level. Needed someone high quality. I told him that wasn't my shib, but I knew someone. So I arranged a meeting with Lydo. We agreed I would get a finder's fee of twenty million. Only I never got it. What showed up in my account was ghost. Gone the next day. I swear there's more honor among gangsters."

"So he screwed you, too," Chris said.

Nicholle took a sip of her soda. "One thing I don't get. Lydo's people have skills. How'd you get a sepsis past them?"

A grin pulled at the edges of Tuma's mouth. "Sometimes it *is* about the money. I've had one of Lydo's programmers on my payroll for about a month. He knew the sepsis was coming and, let's just say, helped it along."

"You sly dog," Nicholle said. She leaned back in the chair and raked her hair with her fingers. "So how do we clear our names and get rid of this Perim?"

"I don't know about you, but I'm getting tired of his shit. We need to open his node for the world to see. Send it to the news wires. By the time they're done, he won't have anyplace to go," Chris said.

"And how do we do that?" Tuma said.

"Lydo's people have skills that would put Homeland Intelligence to shame," Nicholle said.

Chris grinned. "Exactly."

chapter 14

Tiredness and boredom crashed down. Thia squeezed the inside of her knee, calling up a mixture of adrenaline and dopamine. The former to fight sleep, the latter to activate her pleasure center. A mild high. She more than deserved it. Sitting in a dark parking lot beside an abandoned building didn't exactly rock her boat. But she had official sanction to track down Wills Ryder, and she would accomplish that with her last, dying breath, if need be. She would call in all her markers, push the techrus, kick ass, and take names. Whatever it took. Unfortunately, at the moment, it took patience and research.

She was camped outside the obire that Geren Ryder was in. She figured at least one of his children would come to see him. Thia downloaded the images gathered from street cameras for Nicholle's face. She picked several close matches and magnified them. The first showed a woman going into a thrift store wearing a dress with large purple and orange flowers.

"Definitely not Nicholle," Thia said. The next showed a woman walking with two kids into a grocery store.

"Not her, either."

On and on it went, similar eyes, same blue hair, identical build, but nothing that matched all the characteristics.

"Where are you, Nicholle? More importantly, where's your brother?"

She leaned back against the seat, focusing her efforts. If he had tried to contact her, it would show up in the cog records. So that was one marker to call in. She cogged Jefrim Smith, a SIGINT analyst in the INFOSEC department. He owed her a favor.

His image swam up before her, a slack-jawed twenty-something with huge ears and a penchant for wearing the ugliest ties known to man.

"Who?" he said. Doubt tinged his voice.

"It's me, Thia. I've…changed, but yes, it's me."

"How do I know it's you? You look so different. Plastics?" he said.

"Beyond plastics. And it's me because I know you tried to pick up a prostitute in a bar, only it was a Mossad agent who was pumping you for info, and I had to get you out of that bind. You do remember that, right?"

"Thia." He smiled. "What can I do you for?" He munched on a protein bar. His tie askew, the crumbs collected in the small trough that formed just above his pot belly.

"I need a scan on Nicholle Ryder's cogs. Specifically on one from Wills, which will most likely show up as a ghost."

"Ghost? Hm, that might take a while, depending on the integrity of the coherent end system and the quality of the security mechanisms. I mean the kinematical nonlocality—"

"Look, whatever it takes, do it. I don't care about your kinematical whatever. As soon as possible. How long is a while?"

"Day or so, depending on when I get to it. I've got deadlines for two other projects I'm working on for the director. I'm up for associate director of the INFOSEC division." His mouth cleaved to reveal a webwork of tattooed teeth, emblazoned with designs she'd never seen before. Most likely the latest in smartwear. The designs may have served a purpose, or they may have just been decoration. In either case, it presented an unflattering picture. He also had the habit of bragging about his minimal accomplishments. As if she cared.

"Listen, you little shit. I don't care if you're up for Grand Poobah of the Coalition of Square Assholes. You owe me for tracking down that bastard brother of yours. And that took time from three other projects I was working on. So don't give me the runaround. Get to work on it, and get to work now. And cog me when you get the address. I'm waiting by a boarded-up warehouse, so the sooner, the better."

"Well, you don't have to be nasty about it." He sighed. "I suppose I can run it on the 830, cross-reference known ghost addys."

"However." If it presented a challenge, he'd be up for it all the more. But it usually paid to sweeten the pot, as well.

"If you get it to me in the next two hours, I'll throw in a recommendation to the director."

"On the heeb?"

"Yeah." Whatever that meant.

"Jabloosh. Get back witcha." His image blanked out, replaced by the view of graffiti-covered bricks. The words "Hell Reaper" were written in large, rounded letters in the form of flames, which gave off a dying light. "Hell" glowed still, the tips of the flames licking up the wall. "Reaper" was left in darkness. A pitchfork pointed downward, a map for the truly ignorant, or perhaps the unbeliever. Thia shook her head.

Camera feeds scrolled along the side of her visual frame, still searching for the target. All she could do was wait. The adrenaline in her system prevented her from sleeping, so she settled on indulging in a virtual game. She set the perimeter alarm and tapped open the program.

Dropped in the middle of a field. Endless hooded figures appeared around her. Her nostrils filled with the stench of burned, rotting flesh. A howl sounded, wrenched from, supposedly, hell. Outnumbered and outflanked.

"You stupid bitch," one of the hooded figures taunted. "Do you think you can walk out of here with the sacred stone of Yemara? Think again. However, we will be merciful. If you hand it over, we'll kill you quickly. If not, we'll slit your throat slowly, let it drip into the hole we'll dig. You'll drown in your own blood."

"You can try, but see what you'll get for your troubles," she said. The two on either side would be the first to go. She wheeled and caught the one on the right with a flying roundhouse, then threw a jab to the one on the left. He fell back, knocking one other down.

Whoo—

She bent backward. The blade of a battle axe cleared her face by millimeters.

—sh!

As he started to swing back around, she grabbed his arm and kicked him hard in the groin. He doubled over and let slip the axe. She commandeered it and took advantage of his bent-over position. Through the vertebrae, like soft butter.

Schwi—

She raised the axe and caught an upraised sword on the flat side.

—ingclank!

The figure pressed down, bearing all his weight on her axe. His funky breath washed over her face from the darkness of his hood. She held her position for a few seconds, her arms straining, then suddenly twisted out from underneath. He stumbled. She whirled around and cleaved his torso in half.

Thwip!

Pain. The arrow sank into her shoulder blade like a butcher's knife into prime cut. The arrowhead protruded from the front, nestled in her chest like a ruby brooch. Agony bubbled up, the scream catching in her throat. She dropped the axe and sidestepped a kick-jab combination. Snatching the arrowhead, she pulled, bringing the rest of the arrow through her body.

Thunk!

A rock cracked the back of her head. Blood seeped out, trickling down the back of her neck. *Shit*! Her hand came away red. Dizziness rocked her, and she swayed before the hooded figure. She stabbed him in the eye with the arrow, but it passed through him as he dissipated.

A hooded figure swung a mace at Thia's head. Thia ended the game.

Her memory was starting to recover from the trauma of insertion into a new brain. Remembrances of leading Nicholle and a man to a safehouse, to the basement. A bag over her head. Asking for information on her brother. Refusal, then agreement. A node address, then…nothing.

And here she was. On the hunt again in a different body.

"Some crazy whore my brother screwed and dumped? Take a number."

Older memories surfaced.

Candles burned in wall sconces, giving off the scent of vanilla, a hazy glow through the glimmering tulle that covered the bed. His fingers slid across her shoulders and down the crevasse of her spine. They stopped at the base and pressed their way up again, smoothing out the muscles, ridding her of the tension in her back. The buzz from the bottle of champagne cognac still tingled her body.

"Mmm, and I thought the mud bath was heavenly," she said.

"You should try getting in the sauna, then jumping into freezing cold water, back and forth about seven or eight times. That's invigorating," Wills said.

"Sounds like a recipe for the flu."

"On the contrary. You'd be surprised what the body can get used to."

"Well, right now I could get used to this." She rolled over, facing him. The glow of the candlelight blushed his skin with red undertones. She raised a hand to his cheek. He took her hand in his and pressed kisses down the length of her forearm. He stopped at the crook of her elbow. A hooded glance.

"I think you're not just here to seduce me. I think you want a look at my R&D node," he said.

"William, I—" she began. He placed a finger on her lips.

"Shh. It's okay. Just let me peek at yours and we'll call it even.

She was posing as the head of an R&D department for a diode maker. Even had a fake node. So she agreed.

Then he drew her closer and spoke Russian in her ear.

Only later did she figure out that he had traced the false node to her real one. On Homeland Intelligence.

A pinging interrupted the memory. She tapped open the line. Greeted with the tattooed smile of Jefrim. He had wiped away the crumbs.

"Good news. Well, sorta. I ran the scan and found a ghosted call, but it has two sources. One is near you, the other I'm still working on."

"Two? Is that unusual?"

"Somewhat. I've seen it before. Someone's running a patch through someone else's chip. Requires the other person's permission, or an intimate knowledge of their DNA and brain wave patterns. Either way, it ain't easy to come by. This guy went through a lot of trouble."

Or owns a database of people's brain wave patterns.

"What's the address of the one nearby?"

"Two-two-oh Guam Avenue, Northwest."

"Thanks, Jefrim. Consider your debt paid in full."

"Ahem. The recommendation?"

Of course he would remember that. "Ping me a reminder and I'll write it in the morning."

"You'd better."

"Just get that second source." Thia closed the line.

○

She cruised the narrow street, eyeing the mausoleum perched on a postage-stamp yard: 220 Guam Avenue. English tudor adorned the top, field stone on the bottom. Even in the dark, the manicured lawns glowed an eerie green. Enhanced chlorophyll? *What will they think of next?*

Luxury cars hunched in the driveways. Even a stray miniature here and there, a child's toy left to the elements.

She parked two blocks over and changed in the car, windows blackened. Burglary clothes she kept in a hidden compartment under the back seat, along with her tools. Being prepared wasn't only the Boy Scouts' motto.

She placed the tools in hidden pockets on her molded black outfit. She opened up a small square in the floor and eased herself down onto her back. Small wheels extruded from her shoulder blades and calves. Pushing herself along under the row of cars, she made it to the top of the street. She climbed out from under the car and crossed over ten lawns, keeping low and close to large, obscuring objects. Her suit masked against motion detectors, but sometimes the occasional dog would look her way and begin barking, which usually elicited shouts of "Shut up!" from the owners. *If only they knew.*

She finally reached the tudor house. No dog. Initiated a scan: bio-ID, 20-zone, MD, secbots, auto-blasters, SRS, and cameras. *What is he hiding in there? Gold bricks?*

MD. What did that mean? Probably motion detector. Damn her brain. SRS? She seemed to recall Surveillance and Reconnaissance System.

She perched under the patio and waited. High Leyland cypresses framed the yard, blocking the view of nosy neighbors. The house was dark. If the owner was on vacation, she'd be out of luck. Break-in required. She would wait a half hour, then go to Plan B.

Sudoku helped her pass the time. On her third game, a car pulled up in the driveway. Mercedes clicking. Medinites converted her vision to T-ray, cutting through walls and clothing. The figure carried no concealed weaponry. A plus. He walked up the sidewalk and into the front door. She switched back to real sight, crawled around to the side of the house, and peered into the window. The figure was a man. He took off his coat and handed it to a butlyr, which hung it in the closet.

The face looked familiar, but she couldn't place it. Her memory had never been in question before. She could remember names and faces like an airport AI. Damned Eyon. He hadn't wanted to "strain her new brain" by introducing too many foreign engrams, but she couldn't function like this. Her life depended on lightning-quick mental processes. Any breakdown could cause a blackened hole in the middle of her chest.

She scanned the image of the man's face and ran it through national ID. He must have received a cog, because he sat on the couch in the family room and began talking. But she only heard one side of the conversation.

"We'll start layoffs tomorrow across departments. I'll send a list Vedor created based on productivity levels," he said.

"Yes, the police questioned me. I told them Spyre acted on his own for reasons I didn't know."

"His status hasn't changed. You want him sent to Fiji? All right. I'll arrange it."

"No, no sign of Nicholle. Are you sure? Fine, I won't have her killed."

"Yes, I'll be in touch."

The scan results flickered her vision. The man in question: Perim Nestor.

AmHo VP.

Fiji, eh, Wills? So I'm not the only one you're using.

A cog. Jefrim again. "I'm kinda busy right now," she said.

Brilliant light flooded the yard, negating her night vision. Blind. The sound of blasters priming and secbots mounting up sent adrenaline coursing through her.

"I found the other source," Jefrim said.

"Can't talk now."

Instincts forced her to the ground, rolling away from the patio. Blue flare zigzagged, aimed to her previous location. Millimeter-wave energy, designed to instill the feeling of being on fire. She tapped down the night vision, contracting the pupils. The secbots' scan wouldn't detect her form, which would precipitate a wide-disbursal shot. A gutter beckoned.

"The address is four-twenty-seven Wake Island Road, Northeast. What about my recomm—"

"Text it." She ended the call, jumped, and grabbed hold of the gutter. Scrambled up and flattened against the wall, but the disbursal caught the edge of her heel.

Searing pain, as if her foot had caught fire.

Climbed up the rest of the gutter and reached the roof. She straddled the ridge and hobbled along until she reached the other edge. The activity below was concentrated on the right side—for now.

What alerted them?

Perched over the edge and extracted a line launcher from her thigh pocket. Clacking against the far wall meant secbots were on the way up. She shot the line into the front yard of the house next door, then attached the other end to the roof with high-powered anchor bolts. Disbursal shot blew a hole in the roof and pitched her forward. She clawed for the line and slid down, gliding over the cypresses, past a fountain, and onto plush grass. Bounded across the sidewalk and beelined up the street. She went the long way around, not wanting to trip another system with carelessness.

She reached the top of the street two blocks over and slid under the cars. Clacking behind her. *Shit! Don't they give up?* She tapped up the car's engine and it started.

She screwed open the door underneath and climbed in the car. It lit up as the field absorbed a shot from the rear, twisted lines arcing across the windshield. She took off.

○

"SRS stood for Speech Recognition System, not Surveillance Reconnaissance. I almost got my ass fried back there, Eyon. I need more memory."

"Oh, all right. Come in and I'll add it. Have you damaged the body?"

"It's not a body, it's me! Stop talking to me like I'm a test subject."

"Just bring your burnt ass in, bitch," Eyon said.

"Excuse me?"

"I added an aggressiveness program. The new me. You like?"

Everybody wanted to be a bad-ass.

"I'll be in soon, so get whatever you need ready." She winked out.

The map glowed dully against the windshield. She hadn't even remembered how to get to Northeast. Vaguely familiar area, but she figured she should know it like the back of her hand. All of D.C., in fact, if she operated here.

The car eased into the neighborhood and found Wake Island Road. A rundown neighborhood with boarded-up houses and a large construction sign promising luxury townhouses—for the newly rich. Only those with old bank could afford single-family houses in the District.

So he was hiding out in a ramshackle house on the seedy side of town. The inside was probably fixed up, though. *Wet bar with Moribel cognac.*

There were no cars parked along the street, so she made her way over three blocks, where there were at least five rowhouses with livable conditions. Barely livable. No back yards with alarms to worry about here. She walked over to the top of Wake Island and memorized the number of houses down from the top of the street his was. Found a manhole and climbed in. She waded down the sewer until she reached the wastewater drain pipe leading to his house. After the fiasco at Perim's house, she decided not to take chances with an alarm and sent in a Buhg—spider-shaped, armed with a camera, heat sensor, and enough energy for one plasma and one heat-ray shot.

She lifted the thing to the mouth of the drain and switched it on. Its legs telescoped out, and the body rose up and turned. The camera would turn on when it reached the bottom of the nearest toilet. Hopefully it wouldn't be in use.

After several minutes, her view filled with the image of a bathroom wall. Wills did most of his thinking on the toilet. Funny she remembered that.

The Buhg crawled down to the floor and headed for the door. It was closed, but the Buhg flattened out and slid under, then continued on its way. The heat sensors showed black. Nothing alive nearby. The house had been dark when she saw it topside.

Buhg-walking through a house always proved tedious, and tiredness tugged at her consciousness. A nice, fluffy bed would look good right about now. She pinched up a jolt of adrenaline.

If Wills was home, she bet he'd be in the basement to avoid turning on lights that could be visible from the outside. A scan revealed no alarm system, but she didn't trust anything that involved Wills. Any alarm controls were probably in the basement, as well. Was the basement finished? She'd bet no. That meant the Buhg went to the first-floor bathroom. It would have to climb down the steps to reach the basement.

Blueprints. Why didn't she think of that earlier? She queried the central database and they popped up to the right. The bathroom was by the front door, the steps leading downstairs were toward the rear of the house. Wills didn't like pets, so she didn't have to worry over a dog barking at the thing.

The Buhg scuttered across cracked concrete, past old soda cups and fast-food wrappers. It reached the top of the stairs and extended spines along the tips of its legs that allowed it to stick to the underside of each step. Night vision showed only step after step, no lights below. She commanded it to keep descending. It trekked down thirteen stairs until it reached the bottom. Heat sensor picked up a figure three meters away, microphone picked up soft snoring.

That you, Wills? Sensors still detected no alarm system. Perhaps he slept with a lason under his pillow. He'd always been cocky. He was a fair fighter, but no expert in hand-to-hand combat or weaponry. Still, if there was no system, it was all-clear for physical entry. She left the Buhg where it was and climbed out of the sewer. Scurried around the back of the house. Testing her luck, she tried the handle. Locked. *Figures.* She inserted a tension wrench and turned it to the right. The pick came next. Listened for the clicking. Felt for the moving pins. Et voilà. She turned the handle and the door opened. She crept inside, tapped up night vision. The kitchen had no sink or appliances. Just a half-torn island with a cracked countertop.

The steps lay to the left, just beyond the threshold to the kitchen. She pulled a lason and held it up, next to her temple. If her weight creaked the floor, that might be the only alarm he would need. She edged her way around and down the top step. The view from the Buhg still showed a sleeping figure. She couldn't believe her luck.

The steps didn't creak in protest at her weight. She stuck close to the wall. Crack!

The step broke underneath her and she fell through. Metal spokes stuck out, scraping against her metallic rubber suit. If she hadn't been wearing it, her skin would have shredded. Footsteps pounded below. Plasma seared the air above her head. He'd employed a low-tech security measure. And she had fallen for it.

Fortunately, the Buhg had remained in its spot, and she ordered it to shoot a disbursal heat ray. A man screamed and dropped his weapon. She pulled herself from the broken step and trained her gun on the figure at the bottom of the steps.

"Don't move," she said. Putting all her weight on the handrail, she slid down the rest of the way. The figure lay on its back, looking up at her. She holstered the gun he had dropped.

"Who the hell are you?" A man's voice. *His* voice. *At long last.*

"I would say your worst nightmare, but that would be cliché. Let's just say a resurrected friend. Now, get up and turn on the light. Slowly. Or my little friend over there will incinerate your lower half."

He took the time to glare at her before following her orders. The light revealed a plushly laid basement, complete with a fresh-water fish tank. A couch and two chairs faced each other over oak flooring.

"On the couch," she said. He sat, stonily silent, neck muscles tense. She peeled off her head covering and shook out the long braid. No flash of recognition passed over his face.

"Friend? I don't know you," he said.

"But you do. Let me help you. We exchanged R&D node peeks. Only you decrypted mine and stole information from HI that you weren't supposed to have. Ring any bells?"

"Thia," he whispered.

"Congratulations. You get the cigar."

"What happened to you? Where's your—other body?"

He was no doubt angling for an escape, even as he spoke, Thia thought. Always calculating.

"Your sister killed me and cut off my hand, so the boys down at HQ fixed me up with a new body. Amazing, eh? Bet your trials aren't this far along. Takes some getting used to, though. Memory's not what it used to be. But I remembered enough, don't you think?"

"I see. So Nicholle killed you? How?"

"That's something I don't care to talk about. But enough about me. You and Perim seem to have a cozy relationship. Care to share?"

His hands curled into fists. "No."

A blast shot past his ear and seared a hole in the wall behind him. The smell of burning paint and paper.

"That wasn't a request."

His face tensed, throttled-back anger. But he had no choice.

"I'm using Perim."

"I figured out that much. Details, Wills. Where the devil is."

"I patched a ghost through his brain wave pattern, made myself invisible so I could work behind the scenes. But I needed to know what was going on at American Hologram. I still have an interest in the company that needs to be handled."

"And I know you didn't trust Perim to handle it. Compulsive control issues. They're not just for stalkers and wife-beaters anymore. Does Perim do exactly whatever you tell him to?" Thia said.

"In a way."

"How vague. What a good political scandal witness you'd make. Try something more substantial."

"Well, he's like you, actually. My pattern overlaid on his. He thinks like me. I let him keep his memories, though. Didn't want to raise too many suspicions."

Beyond belief. His boundless capacity for greed and self-preservation astounded her. "You took some poor unsuspecting guy and turned him into your twin? You mean lurking under that personality might actually be someone nice?"

Wills shrugged. "I doubt it."

"Why?"

"Because he's my brother."

He took advantage of her shock, leaned to her left and snatched something between the cushion. Threw it at her. A flash-bang. Blazing light exploded, crowding out her vision. She shot blindly, wild, to prevent him from killing her.

When she recovered, he was gone.

chapter 15

Chris and a woman Nicholle hadn't seen before sat at a table near the window of the food court in Tuma's Town Center, crouching over the vestiges of sausage and biscuits. Chris waved Nicholle over. They had decided the night before to get a good night's sleep before cracking Wills' node.

"Nicholle, this is Xelo, arrived last night. She was one of Lydo's programmers, the one Tuma was talking about," Chris said.

Xelo had short blonde hair and a square jawline. Nothing like the walking nightmares that had accosted her at Lydo's.

"But you're..." Nicholle began.

"Normal looking?" She chuckled. "I was one of the leads. We have to interface with the public so we're not wired in like the lowers."

The last pack of eggs and bacon sat under a harsh white light in the vending machine. Nicholle paid and opened the small door to retrieve her prize. Popped the tab and shook the contents. She inhaled the tantalizing scent, but her attention was drawn to a caffeine infuser glittering in the morning sun on the countertop, set for 300. She scurried over and cranked it up to 700. The caffeine tingled her nose. Her tiredness ebbed, giving way to renewed energy. A legal high.

She sidestepped empty chairs to get to Chris's table, then tucked into her breakfast. "You guys map out a plan?"

Chris yawned, shaking his head. "Not yet. I'm running it past Cor, too, though. But we'll start in earnest after breakfast."

Nicholle hung her head. "How is Cor?"

"He only agreed to help cuz it's Wills and it'll give him cred on the versos."

They sat in silence for several minutes, everyone either too tired, too overwhelmed, or too out of ideas to say anything. "Well, I'd better get back at it," Xelo said. "I'll see you guys later."

Which left Nicholle and Chris alone at the table. Two pakzers came in and checked out the vending machine. They began lamenting the fact there were no more bacon and eggs.

Chris reached over and wrapped an arm around her shoulder. He pulled her to him and rested his head on hers. The crook of his neck cradled her face. She hooked her fingers in his shirt pocket.

"How are you holding up?" he said, voice just above a whisper.

"I don't know. Sometimes I wonder when I'll just crack and have to be carried away for extra programming." She paused. "I almost got hooked again last night. Lydo disarmed my medinites and shot me with a pakz. And I have to admit, it felt great. It felt familiar, and I thought I needed that."

She slid her head from its cradle. Their faces inches apart.

"But you know what? The bad memories flooded back, as well. Of being laid out somewhere you didn't remember going to, of fighting over someone else's last pakz that they promised to a friend, of shaking from an overdose, hoping your medinites got the excess out in time. Wondering where your next hit was coming from. It made me not want to be high. And I'd never felt that before."

The two pakzers kept stealing glances at them, whispering between themselves. Chris squeezed her shoulder.

"Come on. Let's go to the room."

✿

Chris locked the door, turning it dark grey.

"Shouldn't you be helping Xelo? I don't want to hog your time if you're needed elsewhere," Nicholle said.

"You wanted to talk, so talk. If you don't, you'll end up needing extra medinite programming to calm you down. And right now I don't have time to cart your ass to an institute. So start talking."

She jabbed his chest, grinning despite herself. "Reemoid."

"And proud of it. So, come on. You didn't want to be high?"

She sat down on the bed. Her legs dangled below. That morning, she had found some old sweats in her drawer and squeezed into them, having gained weight since she'd been sober.

"After I went through rehab, I got a cheat, a fix. I had paid a doctor at the clinic to give me a way to experience a high, suspend the substance-blockers. Just for a moment. Nothing big. But it made me want more. Several times over the past few months, I almost bought pakz, just so I could feel the high for a few seconds. It was hard. I even locked myself in my bathroom once. But then this whole thing happened and I was so worried over my father and the company that I scarcely thought about it. But at Lydo's, all bets were off. It was full-blown addiction in a moment."

She looked up from her feet to Chris's face. He was kneeling in front of her. His eyebrows pangeaed in concern. "Do you know what that's like?" she said.

He edged in between her legs, filling the space between her knees. He touched her cheek, caressed her skin with his thumb. Heat rose up her thighs, igniting at the apex.

His hand brushed back her hair and he gently pulled her toward him, cupping her nape with his palm.

"Yeah, I do," he said. "I'd offer my help, but I don't think you need it." He closed the distance between them and pressed his lips to hers. Gentle, barely touching, a breath caught between them. Then a surge of breath, the kiss more insistent, an urgency that caught her up in its passion. She wrapped her arms around his neck and swung her legs around his waist, hooked her ankles. He slid her off the bed, fingers gripping her buttocks. He leaned back and hoisted her up, until her full weight was on him. His hand wended upward, to the crown of her head, each finger's trail leaving a wake of seething heat.

A chime sounded. The door.

"Damn," she said. Her breath came heavy and fast against his cheek. "I can't win for losing."

"Just ignore it. They'll go away."

He tilted his face up and kissed her again, the same fervor bespoken in his embrace. She fell deeper into his arms.

The door chimed again. "Chris? Nicholle? I have something to show you." The voice belonged to Xelo. *Damn Tuma's cheap magfields.*

Chris set her down on the bed, still nestled between her legs. His chest heaved, breaths ragged.

"She picked a hell of a time to find something," he said. He stood up, pulling his shirt out. It hung down, covering the swelling in his pants. Nicholle stood and smoothed her pants and her hair, adjusted her top.

"I'll get it," she said. She tapped the wall panel. The dark grey of the magfield faded to clarity.

Xelo stepped in. "Sorry, man," she said, sheepishly. "But I was bouncing around on Wills' node and found the server he's running off of, but it's nothing like I've seen."

"Right. I found that out just before...well, we were kidnapped. He's on a DNA server. Can you access it?"

Xelo hunched her shoulders. "Could use some help."

"I'll try, too," Nicholle said. She knew she couldn't provide much assistance, if any at all, but she wanted to help.

Xelo transferred the node image to the room's diodes and the image swam up in the midst of them. She and Chris spiraled in. Pink and red shards of light fell, interlocking, then faded to a bold font: **Cognition Two.**

Chris and Xelo went to work on the admin files while Nicholle poked around the perimeter. An area glowed green that read, "Clinical Trials Data."

What are you up to, Wills?

She accessed the area without encountering any barriers. "That's odd. It should have asked for a passwo—"

"You are the corporeal form," said a voice.

Nicholle exchanged looks with Chris and Xelo, who returned a confused stare.

"What was that?" Chris said.

Nicholle shrugged. "Who is the corporeal form?" She didn't really expect a reply.

"The entity known as Nicholle Ryder."

A chill manifested itself, and a faint cry escaped her throat. She swallowed hard, afraid to ask what was on the tip of her tongue…but she steeled herself.

"Corporeal form of what?"

"Of Cognition Two."

chapter 16

"What do you mean corporeal form?" Nicholle said. She could scarcely believe she was talking to a computer form of herself.

"We share the same brain wave pattern," Cog Two said.

"Whoa, whoa hold on. How did you get my…pattern?"

"Wills Ryder designed the specifications. A female brain uses landmark memory at a higher rate. It aids in reassembling cellular structure."

A glance askew to Chris.

"Why are you reassembling cellular structure?" Chris said.

"I program medinites to rearrange cellular structure to a downloaded personality to achieve brain wave pattern parity."

"Downloaded personality? You mean like…" Xelo began.

"Taking over someone's body. Turning it into you," Nicholle said.

"Transference of consciousness," Chris said. "So she was right."

"Cog Two, do you know what happened to Geren Ryder? Why is he in a coma?" Nicholle said. It was worth a shot. The doctors hadn't figured out what was wrong.

"I am suppressing his frontal lobe, as ordered by William Ryder."

Nicholle closed her eyes, attempting to quell the rage rising within. She strained to control her voice.

"I order you to stop suppressing it"

"Suppression ceased," Cog Two said.

Xelo and Chris stood, looking at her, dumbfounded. She ignored them and cogged her father, praying that he would answer. After three tries, he did. His image materialized, blurry at first, then crystal clear.

His dry lips resembled a mummy's bandages. His eyes, however, shone with an intensity she had never seen.

"N-Nicholle, is that you? What's…happened?" Geren said.

"Oh, Daddy. Wills put you in a coma. I think he was going to use you as a test subject in some experiment on consciousness transfer. You have to see the doctors so they don't euthanize you."

"Nicholle, I have something to tell you," he said.

"I know, Daddy. Henroi told me about Perim. But forget him. Why would Wills do this to you?"

Geren sighed, then tears formed in his eyes.

"I should have told you, but I was afraid of losing you. I had an affair with Perim's mother. It was a hard birth and I went to the hospital to see them. When your mother found out, we had a loud fight. Wills overheard us. Part of it. He didn't know the whole story, as far as I knew. But your mother stormed out. Flew off to Paris. Only…"

He stopped. Nicholle knew the rest. Two dead, her mother and the pilot. Engine failure. Dental records had to identify the bodies.

"Wills blamed me for that. And I couldn't stand to look at him, knowing that he knew. He hated me."

"That's why you were never home," she said. "That's why. And you've known all this time about Perim."

"I disowned them both and fixed it so she'd never get a job making higher than minimum wage so she'd never come after me legally. I'm…sorry, Nicholle," her father said.

Her father had always seemed larger than life before. Rich businessman. Shrewd investor. Pillar of the community. Could do anything, say anything he pleased. And no one would say otherwise. But now—

"Can you walk?"

He swung his legs off the bed and stood up.

"Seems I can." He beamed. "The medi—"

"Good. Get yourself a cab." She closed the call.

"Cog Two, lock out William Ryder's authorization." She turned to Chris. "We need to get to AmHo and find out what the hell's going on."

○

Cog Two had disabled security, or if Nicholle thought about it, she had disabled it. *Too bizarre.* She, Chris, and Xelo headed down the hall toward Wills' office. At one o'clock in the morning, no one was likely to be there. Employees had long since packed up and left, except for the dedicated programmers on the third floor. But they hardly wandered, holed up in their offices, subsisting on toaster tarts and cheese slices slipped under their doors by concerned coworkers.

But voices carried down the hall. "—reasonable." A woman's voice.

"How the hell did you know I was here?" Wills' voice.

"Funny thing about security measures. The more you have, the more unique of an output signature you have. I just followed the trail. Too smart for your own good."

The group walked through a palm frond magfield into Wills' office. Nicholle hadn't expected to see anyone, but she was presented with a family reunion. Perim stood behind a desk, facing Wills, who stood on the other side. A woman held a gun on both of them.

"What are you doing here?" Wills and Perim spoke in unison.

"How sweet. Two peas in a pod," Thia said.

"Who is she?" Nicholle said.

"A friend," Wills said.

"Tsk tsk. Oh, but we were so much more than that." She looked at Nicholle. "Don't you remember? I'm Thia. We met before, when you killed me. Remember?"

"You? But you were—"

"Dead, yes. I got an upgrade."

"Transfer of consciousness," Nicholle whispered. "It works."

"Now all I need are the data from the clinical trials, Wills," Thia said. "Or rather, the government does. And I'll be on my way. We'll get back to you about a percentage."

"You expect me to believe you'll just let me walk out of here?" Wills said. "I don't think so. I need leverage. Patent pending."

"Think again."

She pointed the blaster at him. He ignored her and turned his attention toward Nicholle, smiling at her.

"So you figured it out. Excellent. Now, tell Cog Two to—"

"I'm not doing anything for you, Wills. Do you think I'm going to be in league with you, with death, over money?"

Wills threw back his head and laughed, a resonant tone rumbling in his chest. "That's rich, coming from an ex-drug dealer. Tell me, how many of your customers pakzed out, dying in some abandoned building? Or some skeemzer who had his neurons fried to hell sitting on his bed? A little self-righteous, don't you think?"

"How dare you," she said. The comment cut. Because it was true.

"I dare because I was the one who took you in after you came crawling back, wired out, broke, and filthy. I was the one who cleaned you up."

"I cleaned myself up. I was the one who went through—"

"Spare us all. The only reason you came back was because your pimp got tired of you and set you up. He realized you weren't the moneybags he wanted. Guess you were too wired to know you were being used."

"I knew more than you think."

"Then you're dumber than I thought for putting up with trash like Tuma."

"He's more of a man than you'll ever be."

Wills moved lightening fast. A blur, he grabbed Thia's arm and snatched it forward, catching her off balance. He swung a leg around and she tripped. He caught her and wrenched the gun from her, pointed it at her head. Then he transferred the aim to Perim.

"It's time for you to go, Perim."

Before Wills could aim straight, Perim ducked behind his desk. Wills fired. The top half of the desk charred. Scent of a roaring fire rose up.

Nicholle, Chris, and Xelo dove for the floor. Perim extended a leg and snatched up a lason strapped to his ankle. He fired it at Wills, who was rounding the overturned desk. The blue flare singed Wills' face in half, a scorched V where his right eye had been. But he had already fingered the trigger before he fell, squeezing off another shot. It acquired the target. A thump as Perim's hand dropped. The top of Perim's head showed through the space under the desk—a blackened plateau.

Thia and Nicholle eyed each other, stomachs flat on the ground. Nicholle didn't know whether Thia still harbored murderous tendencies toward her. She tensed.

"Now that's poetic justice," Thia said. "But I guess that means you're president now. So I'll be taking the data."

"Care to negotiate?" Nicholle said.

Thia grinned.

Epilogue

The "Prado in Anacostia" exhibit loomed before Nicholle, Chris, Tuma, and Reya as they stood in the crisp air of an April morning. The line snaked down the riverside, but moved steadily. Children ran and played or fidgeted in line for the carnival rides.

"Now this…is what it's all about," Nicholle said, extending both arms in a grand gesture.

Tuma's color had returned. Nicholle had negotiated probation for him in lieu of drug charges. He'd passed off his empire to Zee, who was forced to jettison the illegal activity, which left him with gambling and prostitution. Still lucrative.

Nicholle had hired Tuma as European Liaison; he had, in his first month, charmed not only the Guggenheim for holographic rights to *Accompanied Contrast,* but the Catherine Palace for the Amber Room.

"I'd love to stay, but I have to get back to the office," Chris said. "Congratulations on the opening."

"All right, Mr. President," Nicholle said, grabbing him by the lapel. "Don't forget we have to view the wedding reception hall at seven."

"That's why I'm heading back to the office, to get some work done so I can leave in time." He gave her a peck on the cheek.

"Bye, Reya, Tuma." He waved and jogged off toward his car.

"Hm, so…" Tuma began. "…what's next? Guggenheim in Glover Park? Hermitage in Herndon?"

"Actually…I'm thinking of the restored city of Thebes with Luxor Temple on the National Mall," Nicholle said.

"Tricky," Reya said. "I'm not sure you'll be able to get approval."

"Oh, there's a Senator McKay who I think would be most enthusiastic about it," Nicholle said. "In fact, make an appointment."

About the Author

Daughter to a U.S. Army father, K. Ceres Wright has lived in Anchorage, AK; Chicago, IL; Baltimore, MD; Frankfurt, Oberursel, and Munich, Germany; Seoul, Korea; and the Washington Metropolitan Area. She attended undergraduate school at the University of Maryland, College Park, with a double major in economics and finance, then worked for 10 years as a credit and treasury analyst before deciding to change careers.

Wright received her Master's degree in Writing Popular Fiction from Seton Hill University in Greensburg, PA, and *Cog* was her thesis novel for the program. An accomplished poet, Wright's science fiction poem "Doomed" was a nominee for the Rhysling Award, the Science Fiction Poetry Association's highest honor. Her work has appeared in *Hazard Yet Forward*; *Genesis: An Anthology of Black Science Fiction*; *Many Genres, One Craft*; and *The 2008 Rhysling Anthology*.

She currently works as an editor/writer for a management consulting firm and lives in Crofton, MD, with her son, Ian, and daughter, Chloe. Visit her website at http://www.kcereswright.com and find her on Twitter @KCeresWright.

CPSIA information can be obtained at www.ICGtesting.com
Printed in the USA
BVOW08s1240160813

328705BV00002B/14/P